D0685208

From the

MOUNTAINS

TO THE

VALLEY

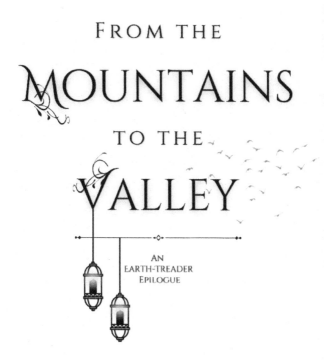

AN
EARTH-TREADER
EPILOGUE

BY ALISSA J. ZAVALIANOS

NOVELS

The Earth-Treader
The Wishing Seed
Endlewood

SHORT STORIES

From the Mountains to the Valley — An *Earth-Treader* Epilogue

FROM THE
MOUNTAINS
TO THE
VALLEY

AN
EARTH-TREADER
EPILOGUE

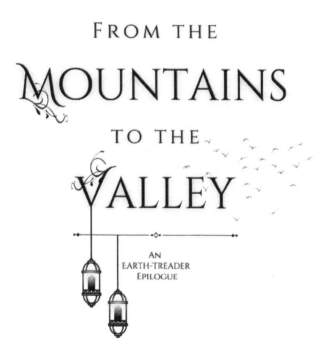

ALISSA J. ZAVALIANOS

Copyright © 2022 by Alissa J. Zavalianos

Printed in the United States of America

Cover by Alissa J. Zavalianos
Map by Chaim Holtjer
Edited by Caitlin Miller

ISBN 9798839045514 (paperback)

*To my fellow Earth-Treaders and those
who love happily ever afters.
This one's for you.*

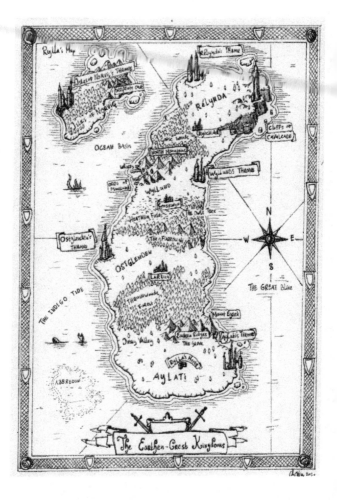

The Earthen-Crest Kingdoms

AN
EARTH-TREADER
EPILOGUE

The Beginning, Or Rather, The End

The smell of fresh rainfall lingered in the air, a herald of springtime and longer and brighter days ahead. Dewy droplets covered the grass and trees, the green sparkling like crystals. Birdsong was its own melody, accompanying the fanfare of a day made beautiful simply by existing.

Rylla peered out from her loft window and squinted at the golden sunlight dancing through the lemon trees, as if waving good morrow and wishing her happiness on the happiest day of her life.

Her wedding day.

After a long time of healing for both her and her brothers, not to mention all the preparations involved, the day was finally here.

A year had passed since Caz got down on one knee, called her as stubborn as a horse (among a myriad of other things), and asked her to marry him. And she loved him all the more for it.

She often replayed that moment in the Grove, wishing she had been strong enough to stay there longer. Defeating Lord Brennigan with the kingdom stones had taken a toll on her body. If it hadn't been for Caz carrying her home, she was sure she'd collapse on the way, causing her parents greater fear.

Still. That day lived perfectly in her memory, untouched. And she had a feeling today would, too.

Rylla pushed off from the windowsill and threw back the covers, the fabric gentle against her scarred hands. After destroying the stones, the soft pink of her skin was now a deep and mottled red. Her hands had healed, but they would never be the same—some wounds ran deeper than others. It was a truth that had been hard to accept at first.

"Scars tell their own stories, Rylla, and I look forward to you sharing them with our future children. Whenever that may come," Caz had said to her one day, taking her hands in his own. He kissed the pinch between her brows and ran a thumb down the side of her cheek before gently cupping her chin. *"There's no shame in bearing your strength."*

A small smile crept up Rylla's face at the recollection. She certainly held no shame now; but she held memory, and that was its own beast—a chapter not yet closed. Still, she'd grown this past year, and for that, she was grateful.

A knock sounded at the base of the loft's ladder.

"Rylla, my Sweet, are you awake?" Her mother's voice drifted up from the ground floor.

Instead of answering right away, Rylla poked her head over the edge of the platform, a wide grin on her face. "It would appear so," she laughed.

"Sleep well?" her mother asked.

"Hardly a wink."

"Then we are more similar than I thought," her mother laughed now, too. It was light and airy and turned into a delighted shriek when Rylla's father came up behind her and planted a kiss against his wife's ear. His cane dropped to the floor beside him.

"What'd I miss?" he asked, humor in his eyes. "Our only daughter hasn't gone off and married that soldier already, has she?"

"Ha ha." Rylla rolled her eyes, not able to keep the delight from her face. "Can't get rid of me that easily, Da."

"And why would I want to? There hasn't been a better cartographer in the family since your great, great gramp passed over thirty years ago. I'm saying goodbye to my prodigy, you know." He winked, embracing his wife affectionately while smiling warmly at his daughter.

The words touched Rylla's heart but saddened it all the same. She'd had a year to plan and prepare for this day, but the thought of leaving her parents hadn't really sunk in. Where would she and Caz live?

She knew one day she'd like to go exploring, and after months of staying at home, the time was nearing. But having an actual home—*that* was more permanent. It mattered much where one ended up at the end of a long journey. And especially who would be around thereafter.

"Do you trust me?" Caz had asked, pressing her hand in assurance as much as he needed her faith in him. He had taken on the role of provider rather quickly and whole-heartedly, tasking himself with finding them a home. Rylla knew how much this meant to him, how sometimes he was still running from his shadows and felt the need to infuse more light in his past by proving himself worthy.

She'd stilled him, running a hand up his arm and stopping once it reached the space over his heart. *"Always,"* she'd said. *"But…"*

"But?" His eyes were searching.

"No more running, Caz. Promise?"

He knew what she meant; they read each other so well.

He'd brought her fingers to his lips, brushing a light kiss against her knuckles. *"No more running."* He nodded. *"I promise."*

And she hadn't worried about him

since. For some reason, Rylla felt that she'd find out the answers to her questions very soon.

"Why don't you come downstairs and we can start getting you ready. It looks like the girls have arrived!" her mother said to Rylla. "And as for you, my love..." She turned to her husband, picking up the fallen cane from off the floor. "It's about time you joined the men." She kissed him sweetly on the mouth.

"What I'd give to watch *you* walk down that aisle for the first time again, Clara," Rylla's father reminisced, holding his wife. "Seems like just yesterday we were mere children falling in love." He kissed her back, this time more soundly, and reluctantly let go to limp toward the door. He paused on the threshold and glanced up at Rylla, a glossy look in his eyes which held the kindest, sincerest affection. "And now it's my little girl's turn."

Rylla's chest constricted. Even from atop her loft, the love from her father was so near and dear. It reverberated in this home, through every person he encountered, through every fiber of the Earthen-Crest kingdoms.

There really wasn't anything like a father's love.

"Merry morrow!"

"Happy wedding day!"

New voices entered the house, drying up any unshed tears.

Rylla's heart now thumped with a new note; her family was here. Finally. After all these months. She hadn't seen any of them since...

Hastily, she grabbed her cloak and threw it over her shoulders before sliding down the ladder. She'd hardly taken two steps before she was locked in a familiar embrace.

"Wow, I didn't expect I'd miss you this much," Elowen said.

"Good to see you too," Rylla laughed. It was so good, actually. She'd missed Elowen's quirks more than she'd realized.

"Congratulations, Rylla!" Mari came around with Gracelynn on her hip, the little girl giving a shy smile. "We're so happy to celebrate your special day."

"Thank you," Rylla said, smiling and introducing everyone to her mother.

Overjoyed to finally meet one of her grandchildren, her mother knelt in front of Gracelynn and engaged Mari in a friendly conversation.

That left Rylla free to talk to Elowen. "So what have you been up to all this time? Tell me everything!"

"Well, I've had poached eggs and dry bread for three weeks straight now."

"I didn't mean *everything*." Rylla rolled her eyes. "How's it been back home?"

"I wouldn't know." Elowen shrugged. "I went back for about two weeks and then moved to Wyllund. I've been there ever since."

Rylla smirked. Jovin was from Wyllund. "Hmm, I wonder why."

Now Elowen rolled her eyes.

"How's *that* been going?" Rylla asked.

A subtle blush blossomed on Elowen's cheeks. It was becoming for her, but more shocking than anything. Elowen never bore her heart if she could help it.

"I'll take that as a good sign." Rylla laughed.

"If you must know, I moved to help take care of Uwan. The old man has more bad days than good, but he's coming around. Swiftlock's been helping him too."

She's living in the Ores?

"Swiftlock?"

"His hawk. I'm staying in the room you and I shared. It's quite roomy now that there's only one person sleeping in it."

"I hardly took up that much space."

Elowen ignored her. "And Jovin stays

in the room he shared with Caz. That man remains as irksome as ever." Yet *that man* couldn't keep the smile from her face.

"I hear irksome men can be pretty irresistible." Rylla had one of her own, whom she loved dearly.

"They can be. Especially when they ask you to marry them."

Rylla's mouth dropped open. "He did not! Elowen! When did this happen?"

Elowen smiled fully now. "About three weeks after Caz asked you."

"And you didn't tell me?"

She shrugged. "I've been keeping it under wraps. The man can hardly take his eyes off me. I don't mind having him wait a bit longer." She winked.

"And how long will that be? The poor man." Rylla laughed.

"Eh, I don't really know. But it won't be forever. I guess I like him too much for that." Elowen chuckled, tugging her bow tighter to her body.

11

"Are you girls ready?" Rylla's mother asked, interrupting their conversation.

Rylla nodded and everyone followed her to her parents' bedroom. There, she paused in the doorway, her breath catching in her throat.

Hanging from a solitary hook above the window was her gown.

She'd already known she'd be wearing her mother's wedding dress, but she hadn't seen the finished product yet. Where there had previously been two simple puff sleeves, there now was a sheer cape of the daintiest material trailing from thin straps off the shoulders. And embroidered on the cape was a pair of symmetrical wings much like those on her blue cloak. It was perfect, or very nearly so.

"I love it," Rylla said, fingering the material and watching it catch the morning light. So many fittings. So many alterations. And it finally led to this moment.

"It looks like something you'd wear," Elowen said, casting aside her bow and quiver and fiddling with the straps of her own bag.

"The seamstress finished just early this morning. It took her months to find the right fabric and design, but it all paid off in the end, don't you think?"

"It looks marvelous," Mari said.

"What's this, Mommy?" Gracelynn asked, holding up a large envelope that was sitting on a chair beneath Rylla's dress. "It has a funny mark on it."

Rylla stifled a laugh. It wasn't a mark, but her own name, written in the nearly illegible scrawl of her father's hand. He may be a cartographer, but he always left the lettering to Rylla; his strong suits were landmarks and topography, not the written word.

She took the envelope from Gracelynn, ripping open the wax seal. Inside was a folded piece of canvas and a small letter. She went for the letter first.

Unfolding it, her heart instantly warmed.

> *My dearest Rylla,*
>
> *If you're finally reading this, today is your wedding day. And if I'm a smarter man now than when I first wrote this letter, I'm nowhere near you while you're reading it. Call it a father's intuition, but tears now shed of their own volition—ever since you kids were born. And especially since I knew I was having a little girl.*
>
> *You'll understand one day.*
>
> *For now, it's one step at a time. You're getting married! I've both dreaded and looked forward to this day ever since I first held you in my arms. When your hazel eyes stared back into mine, I knew no man could love you as dearly as I do. I'd be hard-pressed to find a man worthy*

enough to try.

But if you're reading this (which, by now, I'm assuming you still are), then it means someone has succeeded. That you're marrying someone who you've come to love, making him worthy of your affections, for that, in my opinion, is the only way someone can be worthy of you. Because you freely and willingly have given him your heart.

I pray, my dear Rylla, that your future holds a lifetime of joys and adventures, the kinds I get to share with your mother.

And no matter where your new love takes you, remember that I love you more than you'll ever know, and you're never too far away to come back home.

You'll always be my little girl, Love, Your Father (Da)

Tears trickled down Rylla's face, an ember of comfort and assurance warming her middle as she unfolded the piece of canvas next.

Familiar trees and mountains dotted the paper, steep curves for landmasses and detailed landmarks added the finishing touches. There was even a compass rose, set off to the right of the kingdoms and surrounded by The Great Blue. And there, a red heart placed around the Wayscot house with the word *home* sketched above it.

Our map. Rylla's chest swelled.

A piece of paper was clipped to the top of the map with an additional line of familiar scrawl.

P.S. I hope you don't mind. I took the liberty to finish it. I think you'll appreciate the added addition. XO

She knew exactly where to look. To

the left of Aylati, floating in the Indigo
Tide, was now a subtle land mass marked
Abbredun. The legend of old come to life.
A place still sunken below the tides and yet
as real as the very birds in the sky.

As her heart continued to burst with
gratitude, a sliver of excitement thumped
in her chest. It would take an undeniably
strong Water-spell to dive that deep and for
that long. She wasn't sure her lungs could
do it, but maybe some day she'd like to
give it a try.

"He's been eager to give that to you
ever since he finished it." Her mother
placed her hands on Rylla's shoulders,
squeezing gently. "But don't get any ideas
of running away to chase another
adventure just yet," she teased. "Let's get
you married first."

Rylla smiled, and the rest of the
morning proceeded as usual, her mother
singing joyfully. The ladies all donned
their dresses, and even her neighbor,

Winnie, came over to join in the festivities. A light breakfast was served, and Rylla counted down the hours until she'd see her Caz once again.

***

"How does this look?" Caz spread his arms wide as he looked at the men around him. He didn't have much when it came to nice clothes, and what he did have, he had lugged over from Thrushwoode, making Rembrandt more a pack mule than anything.

They were getting ready in the lemon grove, far enough away to not see into the cottage and yet close enough to hear Clara singing. From the months of getting to know Rylla's family, he'd soon learned that her mother lived her life as a lark, from providing every homely comfort for her family and flitting from one task to the other, all the while singing.

18

Much like she was this morning:

Two hearts become one
Beneath the noonday sun
On this blissful wedding day.

Entwined are the hands
Where there lie the bands
On this wistful wedding day.

A kiss thou hath sealed
The vows like a shield
On this wishful wedding day

The words made his chest feel light. Today was the day. He'd be marrying the girl he was crazy about, and it couldn't come fast enough.

"Yeh look like yeh lost a fight with the local tailor. But except for punching yeh, 'e just gave yeh black and blue clothes." Jovin laughed.

"If I had known you needed a suit, I'd

have brought mine," Garth said, not even bothering to comment on just how bad Caz looked.

"If it's any consolation, it all looks the same to me," Finn said, shrugging.

Caz groaned inwardly. This was *not* how he had envisioned this morning. If he had it his way, he'd whisk Rylla to the top of Mount Egret and get married there, shirt or no shirt. What was the point of matching clothes anyway?

He sighed. No. He couldn't do that to her. Her family meant more to her than anything.

"You're in luck, son," Rylla's father said, holding up a finger. He had a knowing gleam in his eyes. "Figured you could use a little help this morning."

He limped to a tree and rounded its backside. When he reappeared, in his hand he bore a jacket and pants of a russet brown color, both completely matching the other. "Why don't you give these a go? I used to be about your size when I was married, though not quite as tall, I'm afraid."

Caz accepted the clothes gratefully. "These were yours?"

"A bit outdated I suppose, but if you're like me, you care more about what happens after the wedding, not all the frivolity."

Caz's cheeks heated at the implication.

"A lifetime of wedded bliss, my boy." He clapped Caz on the shoulder. "Clothes and styles may change with time, but a love that endures…well, that's what sticks around for the long haul. Even through the bickering and arguments."

Caz nodded. "Thank you, Anders."

He squeezed Caz's shoulder again before limping off.

It was going to be a good day.

***

"It's nearly time to go!" Rylla's mother said, clapping her hands together.

"Everyone looks beautiful, and Rylla my Sweet, you look positively ethereal."

Her curls were smoothed around her face, hanging down to her mid-back. Her dress felt as light as a dandelion weed, just waiting for the wind to scatter its seeds. Rylla was thrilled, if not a bit nervous.

Many villagers were expected to attend, not to mention more of her family. She'd finally see her brothers again after almost a year; she'd worried about Garth's wound and Finn's recovery since the day she arrived back home.

Suddenly, something black and white leaped onto the windowsill in her parents' room, with two green eyes reflecting the sun's light.

"Moo!" Rylla ran over to the window and scooped him up into a hug. "I was hoping you'd come!"

Moo, not one to enjoy being held, relaxed against her chest. "I wouldn't miss this day for an entire barrel of catmint,

Rylla." He pulled back and she let him sit once more on the ledge. "You look radiant, like the sun."

Rylla beamed, too overcome with words.

"What did he say?" Elowen asked her.

"That she's the sun," Winnie answered instead. The now eight-year-old girl with blonde curls stood at least an inch or two taller than when Rylla had first left. Her shyness was still there, but it was coupled with an insatiable curiosity to explore the world. "At least, I think that's what he said."

Rylla looked at Winnie, knowing more than the young girl could fathom. *In time, she'll learn her gift. She'll finally make sense of all the voices she hears.*

"Good to see you again, cat." Elowen tipped her light-brown head, the braid swinging from her shoulder before settling once more against her pale-green dress. She looked vulnerable without her bow strung to her back, but Rylla thought it fitting. Wasn't today a day for new beginnings?

Mari was dressed in a deep plum to offset Gracelynn's soft violet. Winnie wore forest green, and Rylla's mother was in a shade of yellow that matched the cottage exterior.

Looking back at Moo, Rylla saw something white strapped around his neck that she hadn't noticed before. It almost blended in with his coat.

"Moo, is that a bow?"

If cats could blush, Moo was very close to it. He brought his head low and began licking his paw, making it more difficult to see.

"It is, isn't it! Whose idea was it? Jovin's?" She knew the man would be around to see Caz get married; the two were like brothers after all. And putting a bow on a cat seemed like something he would do.

Moo glanced up, a glint of humor in his gaze. "I would have liked to see him try."

"Caz, then?"

Moo nodded. "He seemed to think it would be a good idea. I almost clawed him when he reminded me it was the day of your nuptials... like I'd ever forget that." Moo flicked his tail. "I think he's just nervous."

"Nervous?" Rylla's stomach flipped. She knew the feeling well.

Elowen glanced at her, shrugging. "No. It's not like I'm the one getting married."

"I wasn't..." Rylla looked from Moo to her sister-in-law. "Never mind."

"Everyone ready? Rylla?" her mother asked, making special eye contact with her. "The men should already be there."

"Speaking of," Moo chimed in. "I should claim my post. See you soon, Rylla!" He jumped from the sill and bounded in the other direction.

It was time. She was going to marry Caz.

***

The walk to the Grove felt different now than all the other times Rylla had ventured there prior. This time she wouldn't be making camp with her brothers, nor would she be tasked with saving the kingdoms—at least, she hoped not. Today, she'd be pledging her life to another, making good on her vow.

It was strangely surreal. Here she was now, nineteen years old and hopefully wiser, when only a year ago she had first set out on her perilous quest. Time moved of its own accord, often softening the dredges of the past.

Rylla gathered the fabric of her white dress in her hands as she carefully stepped along the dusty road. She held her head high and breathed in the fresh afternoon air; it invigorated her bones and set her heart ablaze with anticipation.

"Rylla! Your shoes!" Mari gasped, causing everyone to stop just before reaching the forest path. Gracelynn sucked on her bottom lip while holding her mother's hand, and Winnie was nearby trying not to giggle.

"What about them?" Elowen asked, and when she looked at the space below Rylla's hem, she crossed her arms over her chest, lifting a brow.

Rylla's cheeks heated. She hadn't meant to bring attention to her feet. "Oops. I must have forgotten."

But the look on her mother's face was filled with a secret knowing. She couldn't get Rylla to wear shoes even on the worst of days, let alone a day filled with birdsong and sunshine. It had been a miracle at all that Rylla had donned boots when she left a year ago.

"A true forest bride," her mother said. "Wouldn't have expected it any other way." She squeezed Rylla's hand affectionately. "But we must hurry. I hear the music; they're expecting us."

The group of girls moved through the forest like fairies, the littlest ones leading the way with Rylla and her mother in the back.

Just where the forest path was about to open up into the rest of the Grove, Rylla spotted her father, standing at the ready. He looked modestly dressed in a simple cotton shirt, and he'd even combed his hair.

"Hi, Da." Rylla grabbed his hand while the rest of the women scooted on ahead. The sound of a fiddle and chirping echoed just beyond the trees, and she knew that once she rounded the corner, she'd be seeing Caz.

"My little girl." He touched a hand to her cheek. "You look so beautiful, Rylla."

A sheen of tears lingered in his eyes, but he sucked in a breath, allowing her to link her arm through his. "You ready?"

Rylla nodded, swallowing the lump in her throat. Her chest was tight, and yet, lighter than it had ever been.

A step forward, and then another, and the Grove opened up in all its splendor.

Rylla tried hard to keep her mouth from falling open, for there were countless pinpricks of light amidst the dark green of the canopy. Had Caz hired fairies to light the trees?

And there, just overhead, perched the Great Owl in a nearby oak. His piercing silver eye gleamed with wonder and knowing, and Rylla could have sworn she saw him smile. He was surrounded by a host of birds, many of whom she recognized from before. The owl bowed his head before speaking softly, "The merriest of sentiments upon this momentous occasion, Lady Rylla."

She bowed her head subtly and scanned the rest of the attendees, spotting Uwan near the middle, a Red-tailed Hawk perched on his shoulder. Jovin and Elowen sat just to his right. And there was that guard who had captured Rylla when crossing the Ocean Basin—Gordon, was it? Or maybe Gorvo?—and a woman sat beside him, holding his hand.

To the left she spotted Garth and Mari with their children, and then Finn and their mother. Many villagers had come, and there were even a few empty seats left in memory of those who had passed. It was a family reunion of the ages, a dream.

She finally brought her gaze to the front where Fang and Moo sat to the left of the wedding arch, their manes puffed out in all their regality. Both dipped their heads in acknowledgement, Moo looking eager to run to her if not for Fang's steadying paw on his own. A fiddler played just behind them, a soft, lilting tune that wrapped the entire Grove in its embrace.

And then she saw him.

Caz.

His gaze bore right through hers, a look of deep longing in his honey-brown eyes. They were glossy, and Rylla nearly choked when she saw a tear trickle down his cheek. Caz was known for being serious, but right now, Rylla had never seen him smile so wide. It was almost enough to undo her.

Rylla nearly tripped, but her father tightened his grasp on her arm, keeping her from falling.

"Thanks," she whispered.

"None of that face-planting business on your special day." He patted her hand.

Sudden gasps sounded behind them, enough to combat the strings of the fiddle. Curious, Rylla glanced over her shoulder.

The path she had walked from the mouth of the Grove to where she now stood was glistening. The blades of grass were no longer green, but a shimmering and ethereal gold.

"What magic!"

"An Earth-Treader for sure."

"Are the stories true then?"

"The legend of old!"

Rylla smiled at the murmurings. Many of the villagers had heard the tales, but there were still a few who refused to believe. She assumed that's why many of them even came to her wedding at all. To see for themselves the supposed "Earth-Treader" who had saved their realm.

Well, let them come. They'll learn not to fear.

The trail of gold continued to follow in Rylla's wake, a blanket of promise and of brighter things to follow.

Rylla neared her betrothed, and once she made it to the front of the aisle, Caz stepped forward, taking her hand from her father's.

"Treat her well, son," her father said.

"You have my word." Caz nodded, bringing Rylla toward the middle of the arch.

There, the village priest stood waiting for them, his white cravat a stark contrast against his navy shirt and pants.

He cleared his throat and the fiddler ceased his playing. "Dearly beloveds, we are all gathered here today, beneath these boughs, with two-legged and four-legged friends as our company."

Some chuckles resounded in the back, and Rylla noticed Moo puff out his chest even further.

"Today, we are witnesses to these two, Rylla Wayscot of Aylati and Caz of Ostglenden, getting married before our Maker. The two shall become one."

Rylla felt Caz's hands tighten on her own. She was sure many of the attendees didn't miss the lack of Caz's surname. From his time in the orphanage and then in King Grievon's army, he hadn't acquired a true heritage. There were no traces back to his birth family even in Oatglenden's annals. That was another reason why his shadows often tried to claim any of his happiness.

"Aside from my heart, I don't have much to offer you, Rylla. Not a home, not even a last name," he'd said a few days after their engagement, running his hands through his brown locks.

"Don't you see? That's all I want, anyway. But if a family name is what you want to give me, then let's create one together."

The village priest continued, urging Rylla and Caz to exchange vows and rings. A gentle breeze blew in the Grove, tousling Rylla's curls and lifting the cape up from her shoulders before settling it back down once again.

Caz leaned in and whispered into her ear. "You're so beautiful."

Heat climbed Rylla's cheeks, and she

felt her smile widen of its own accord. Any words would betray her if she dared speak again.

"And now, I present to all those in attendance, Caz and Rylla, the new Mr. and Mrs. Dumount."

Mr. and Mrs. Dumount—*from the mountains*. A fitting name, for that's where their hearts belonged after all.

"You may now kiss your bride."

Caz wasted no time.

Rylla's heart soared, and she wrapped her arms around his neck as he lifted her from off the ground. The blades of grass tickled her toes, and she'd never felt so alive.

A chorus of claps erupted while the fiddler struck up another tune, this one livelier than the one prior. It spoke of merriment and celebration. Of their promise that would last a lifetime.

Suddenly, Rylla felt something alight upon her head. When she looked skyward, a host of songbirds hovered just above her, twittering their congratulations. She reached a hand up and felt their gift laden with soft petals and rounded twigs. She pulled a sprig loose, and a large, coral bloom rested in her palm, a poppy of the most beautiful shade.

"A wreath of flowers?" A bubble of laughter escaped her lips. She marveled at the sight.

"I hope you don't mind. I had a word with the owl. I wanted to surprise you." Caz searched her eyes.

"First Moo's bow, then the lights in the trees, and now this? You've done more than surprise me!" Rylla beamed.

"Well, there's still one more thing."

"Congratulations, sister!" Garth's voice carried over to them.

"But I'll wait until later. For now, let's enjoy our company." He winked, pressing a kiss to her forehead before greeting the rest of the family.

***

By the time evening came around, most of the chairs were removed from the Grove and the lights in the trees had increased ten-fold. Instead of just one fiddler, there were now three, and a table filled with juice and homemade pastries sat off to the side.

A large bonfire burned in the center of the Grove, a circle of chairs around the glowing warmth. And seeing as most of the villagers had gone home, it left the Grove to the newly wedded Dumounts and their close family and friends.

"What a day, 'uh?" Jovin said, moving his arm so it draped behind Elowen's chair.

Rylla noticed the subtle way he stroked her shoulder with his thumb.

"Went even better than I'd planned." Caz chuckled, squeezing Rylla's hand.

Caz was a planner to a fault. Sometimes he missed what was right under his nose because he looked too far ahead. Like the time when he'd thought Rylla a lost forest maiden rather than the girl he'd tracked from the Grove.

She smiled at the thought, leaning into his arm. "It was the perfect day."

"Nothin' like sweet marital bliss. Could use a dose of that myself," Jovin said.

Elowen whacked him soundly on the arm.

Jovin laughed. "That's my girl."

Rylla surmised it wouldn't be long before Elowen actually let Jovin marry her.

The group continued to chat, but Rylla's attention was suddenly drawn toward the ground. She pulled away from Caz and leaned forward in her chair.

Moo and Fang slowly approached her, and in Fang's mouth was a wooden box.

He dropped it into her lap, looking up into her eyes. "Merry wedding day, Earthie. Will the wonders never cease?" A glint of humor shone in his orange and teal speckled gaze.

"I supposed not." Rylla smiled. "Should I open it?" She fiddled with the box in her hands.

"Please." Fang dipped his head, and Moo was beside himself, nearly wriggling into a frenzy.

"Hurry up, Rylla!" he said, clearly very excited.

Rylla lifted the lid and peered inside. Her breath caught in her throat.

Laying on a smooth patch of birchwood was a stone. It was of a medium size, and when she took it out, it fit in the palm of her hand. It shone as a soft pink, nearly red in the light of the fire, with orange swirls throughout.

Rylla's heart raced. She'd never seen a stone like this before. Her mind instantly flashed back to her time on the Cliffs, of searing heat before a blinding light. Of Lord Brennigan's shrill cry before all went black.

"What is it called?" She swallowed, worried to be holding another kingdom stone in her grasp. She thought they were all destroyed. She wasn't ready to face any more peril.

"A Seeing Rhodolite," Fang began, reading her nervous expression. "It's a common stone, though not many are found here in Aylati. Perfectly harmless, I assure you."

Rylla released a shaky breath. It was beautiful, almost too beautiful to accept.

Fang continued. "As for its name, well…it's slightly misleading. When holding it, you don't technically *see* anything, but it allows you to hear. And if someone has a matching one, they can hear you back. Two are needed in order for this type of stone to work."

It was then that Rylla looked at Fang's neck. Around his mottled brown and black pelt was a necklace made of twine, and weighing it down hung an identical stone to the one Rylla held in her hand.

"You see, Earthie, now that you're married, there's no knowing where your adventures may take you. And seeing as I can't leave this forest…" Fang's voice grew brusque, as if choking on a crack. "This will keep us connected."

Rylla was off her seat and hugging Fang within seconds. Would the surprises never end on her wedding day?

"Thank you, Fang. Truly, I don't know what else to say." Tears stung her eyes.

"Save your words for the stone. Whenever you're far away from the Grove, I'll always be here to listen, if need be." He placed a paw on her shoulder and pressed his nose to her forehead, marking her as one of his own.

And then he moved away and

disappeared back into the forest, Moo lingering behind.

"Isn't it great, Rylla?" he asked.

"It's wonderful! I can hardly believe how magical this whole day feels."

"Well, you're an Earth-Treader after all. It's only fitting," Moo said.

Suddenly, a deep, low hoot called into the night, and Rylla recognized it as the Great Owl's. He was singing a far-off melody, one without words, and yet she knew it was the signal for the birds to return home. It was a long journey from Aylati to the Owl's Tree.

"Seems many are retiring early," Rylla yawned. "The festivities are almost done, and then all will be back to normal on the morrow, I suppose."

Moo looked at her, tilting his head. "You sound sad."

"Not sad, no. Just…" Rylla bit her lip, thinking. "Everyone's here together *now,* and I wish I could bottle this moment up and keep it with me forever. It's bittersweet, Moo. I am impossibly happy, and yet, I know my life is changing."

Moo nodded, looking Rylla deeper in the eyes. "Family is family, though. And friends are as good as family, too. That won't change."

His words brought comfort, assuaging the fragile places. It was true, the love they all shared wasn't going away, no matter their proximity.

"And besides, wherever you go, I'm going with you," Moo continued.

Her chest felt infinitely lighter. "Are you in earnest?"

"Not even Caz's horse could keep me away. Just promise me the beast won't eat my catmint."

Rylla snorted and couldn't keep from laughing when Caz glanced in her direction. His quirked brow was ridiculously endearing, especially since he had no idea what they were talking about.

"I'll be sure to teach Rembrandt his manners."

They continued to converse, but after seeing Rylla's family start dancing, Moo decided to follow after his grandfather. "I'd prefer not to get trampled. I'll see you in the morning!"

Pretty soon Rylla was dancing in Caz's arms, the bittersweetness of the day melting away with each turn about the fire. She held the train of her dress in one hand and placed the other on her husband's shoulder.

Husband. Would she ever get used to saying that?

The fiddlers struck up a familiar Aylatian tune, typical of marriage festivals and the like. One of the fiddlers even broke away and began singing, his words stirring the air around her.

Strike up the chord and join the song
This dancing day, this dancing day

Come all ye folks, let's sing along
This dancing day, this dancing day

Two hearts now one, what joys it brings
This dancing day, this dancing day
Such wedded bliss is a merry thing
This dancing day, this dancing day

Partners spun around the fire: Rylla
with Caz, Garth with Mari, Jovin with
Elowen, sweet Winnie with Gracelynn,
Rylla's parents... Only Finn sat by
himself, bouncing baby Tobie on his knee.
Uwan sat across from him, a bird on his
shoulder and a smile on his lips as he
clapped his hands to the tune of the music.
Though he couldn't see anything, he was
enjoying the merriment nonetheless.

On seeing her brother sitting alone,
Rylla whispered into Caz's ear. He nodded
and broke away, taking a turn dancing with
Rylla's mother instead, giving her father a
much-needed break off his bad leg.

45

Rylla hadn't seen or talked to Finn ever since that day on the Cliffs. She knew he'd suffered a lot, that he'd also sacrificed a lot, too. But she'd yet to talk to him about it all.

After the wedding ceremony, she'd been able to catch up with Garth. He showed off his wound—just another addition to his already beat-up chest—and they shared a good laugh about it. He'd hugged her and assuaged all her previous fears.

But Rylla had a feeling Finn bore scars one couldn't see.

As she approached him, he looked up, a small smile lifting the corner of his mouth.

"Congrats, Rylla." He rocked Tobie more gently now, the baby's eyes heavy as if plagued by sleep.

"Thanks." She sat down next to him, her gaze taking in the festivities. Winnie twirled Gracelynn around five times, and the little girl's squeals could be heard from where she sat. Fireflies danced between couples, and everyone seemed so blissfully happy.

Everyone that is, except Finn.

Rylla bit her lip, not knowing how to express all that was on her heart. There was an ache there, lodged somewhere deep, the kind that only a sibling would understand.

"I'm all right," he said, answering her unspoken question. "I know that's what you came to ask."

Rylla shifted in her seat and faced him more fully. She took in his appearance, the way the fire cast shadows on the hollows of his cheeks (making him look gaunter than he actually was) and the dark circles under his eyes. He didn't look *all right* at all.

"Truly?" she asked. She wanted to believe him, but she already knew the truth.

Finn looked away, staring off in the

distance, almost as if he were looking through the dancers and to the dark forest beyond. He swallowed, the jaunty strike of the fiddles a direct contrast to his more somber expression. Silence hung heavy in their small corner of the world. "I still think about them."

Rylla's hands trembled beneath the folds of her dress. *Them?*

"They're there when I close my eyes. Behind every dream." He shifted Tobie's sleeping body to lean against his chest more comfortably, but he still didn't take his gaze from the trees. "Sometimes, I can still feel them in my hands. Like they remember…"

Her hands twitched as if filled with a memory of their own.

She had a funny feeling he was talking about the stones. Her chest cracked, an ache so acute; she understood. Though Rylla had never been overpowered by Lord Brennigan's dark magic, she too had held the Earthen-Crest stones. She too had felt their power course through her veins.

"Finn?"

Her brother finally broke his trance-like gaze and met hers, his eyes glistening in the light of the fire. He didn't say a word, but the truth was written on his face. He was suffering, though try as he might hide it.

She knew no words could assuage his hurt, but maybe she could show him he wasn't alone.

Rylla turned her hands facing palm up and laid them out for her brother to see. They looked even worse amidst the reds and oranges of the flames.

Finn's eyes widened as his brain seemed to register what he was seeing. "Was that... Did they..." He couldn't seem to find his words. "What happened?"

Rylla took a deep breath. "That day I defeated Lord Brennigan, he didn't..." She paused. "Sometimes sacrifice doesn't leave us without scathing. I was marked, too."

Rylla's mind traced back to all those sleepless nights of her own. Replaying the events from her battle on the Cliffs. The nightmares had lessened as of late, but still, they haunted her mind every time she glanced at her mottled skin. Yes, there was no longer any shame, but her hands held memories. Not only in their appearance but in their touch. Even now, it felt as if she could still feel the stones.

"You're not alone, Finn. Your battle is mine, too. But there's no shame in bearing your strength." Rylla felt funny quoting Caz, they were his words after all, but they had helped her more than he'd realized.

"What strength, Rylla?" Finn almost barked but remembered to keep his voice low because of Tobie. "There's no strength in feeling weak. In wanting to crumble when all your soul feels is longing. To have what you no longer can, even when you know it's wrong for you. Maybe it's appropriate that all the world has gone black and white."

Rylla blanched. "What do you mean? Black and white?"

"I'm color blind. It might not seem like much, but there's nothing more depressing than not seeing the blue of the ocean or the hue of someone's eyes."

Her chest tightened, and she fought the urge to spill her tears. His hurt went deeper than she'd ever imagined.

Finn sighed. "I'm a broken man, Rylla, but I've learned to accept it. With seeing everyone all together and happy again… Well, let's just say some days are harder than others."

She nodded her understanding and lifted her gaze to the canopy, letting out an exhausted breath. The countless lights from the trees parted enough for Rylla to observe a sliver of sky poking out underneath; the sight smote her chest upon seeing the stars. Their Maker didn't spare any extravagance this night, though she knew the beauty could have just as easily been shrouded by clouds.

People are much the same, she thought. Sometimes they focused too much on the clouds surrounding them that they neglected to see the light that showed through. Not all was darkness.

Rylla cleared her throat, still looking at the stars. "You might be broken, Finn, but that doesn't mean you can never live as whole. There are many who've had much taken from them, and yet, they choose to live in spite of their limitations." She brought her gaze low and watched the dancers once more. "Take Da, for example. And Uwan."

Rylla and Finn watched the men. Their father was dancing once again with his wife, his limp barely visible amongst the flutter of her skirts. And there was Uwan, dancing with Elowen while Jovin laughed heartily. Both men with disadvantages and hurts that most likely went deeper than what could be seen, and yet, they pressed on. They chose to *live*.

"If anyone understands, Uwan will. I'd encourage you to talk to him." He'd been mastered by the Obsidian much like how Finn had been mastered by the Bloodstone. "And I'm here, too." Rylla squeezed Finn's hand and stood up.

She didn't think he'd say anything, but she was caught off guard when he squeezed her hand back.

"Thank you," he choked, clearly trying to hide his emotion. "For everything."

Rylla nodded, trying to keep her own emotions at bay.

What was it about weddings that heightened all her feelings on an astronomical level?

She didn't feel like sitting anymore, nor did she feel like dancing. She needed to move, her body restless and exhausted.

Suddenly, strong arms wrapped around her middle and lifted her off her feet. A gentle kiss pressed against her ear, and a laugh escaped her lips.

"Just the bride I was coming to find," Caz said in her ear.

"Oh really?" Rylla giggled, thankful to be in her husband's embrace once again.

"Yes, I was just thinking… I haven't given you your last surprise yet."

Rylla had almost forgotten! Caz had already done more than enough to make this day special for her, and she couldn't possibly fathom what else he had up his sleeve.

"Come with me."

***

Equipped with a torch, Caz led Rylla away from the dancing and fire. They exited the Grove and took to the dusty road, the brilliancy of the night sky stretching over them like a blanket. The stars were filled with a certain vehemence tonight, as if they knew something special was afoot.

Or at least, that was Caz's hope. He'd spent so many months on this project, he just hoped it paid off.

"Where are you taking me?" Rylla asked, clutching his hand in the darkness, the small light of the fire guiding them forward.

"You'll see."

Caz led her along the road and then turned to the right, veering off the path.

"Town is that way," Rylla said, pointing in the direction they had abandoned.

"I know." He winked, pulling her along even further.

They walked a familiar path, and Caz kept glancing over at her to see if it registered. But whether it was too dark or marital bliss was blinding, she remained oblivious.

Caz was only too thankful, or else it might spoil the surprise too soon.

"How much longer?"

"Just a few more minutes, and then we'll be there." He guided her along a freshly cut path, making sure to keep the torch in front of them so they didn't trip.

His heart sped up when he saw the location emerge in the near distance. They were here. Only a few more steps now.

"Are we headed to the Ivory Valley?" Rylla asked, her brow lifted up in surprise.

"Perhaps."

"We are! I can see it with my own eyes," Rylla laughed. "But what surprise would we find in this abandoned place?"

Caz's heart dropped, but he steadied himself. She didn't realize what he was giving her. She didn't yet know the significance. He only hoped she'd be happy.

Caz led her past the first gristmill, and

they wove their way deeper into the heart of the valley. Finally, after a few more paces, he paused in front of one of the mills. He lifted the torch even higher and loosened his grip around Rylla's waist.

"Surprise!" Caz said, his voice uncertain even to his own ears.

Rylla looked from him to the mill building, a look of shock crossing her features. "Is this…? Is this for me?" She looked speechless.

He nodded. "Come, I'll show you." Caz took the torch and lit the lanterns hanging on either side of the doorframe. The dark blue of the exterior looked almost black in the night, but he hoped come morning, it would look cheerier.

He took out a key from his pocket and unlocked the yellow door before pushing it open. Once inside, he lit more candles and brightened the entire space. A wooden staircase greeted them warmly, as did a hallway and small kitchen to the right.

There were more rooms to see, but they were around the back and upstairs Rylla would have some exploring to do.

Caz glanced at his wife as she stood on the threshold, silent. Her mouth gaped open as she took it all in, and he couldn't quite tell if she was mad or not.

"Do you recognize it?" he asked.

"Am, am I supposed to?" Rylla found her tongue, swallowing.

"It's the old gristmill you fled to the night we first met. The one I entered and you hid in. Remember?"

A light seemed to dawn behind Rylla's eyes as she scanned the place more soundly.

She walked briskly to the kitchen and poked her head in the adjoining rooms. "It's all furnished. And there's not a broken window or a speck of dust!" She looked bewildered. "How long have you worked on this?"

"I may have spent most nights here."

Caz rubbed the back of his neck, watching her closely. He was almost afraid to ask what she thought. He'd worked so hard to give her a home, to give her a place close by to those she loved most. "You really should see it in the daytime. I think you'd like the flowers, and with the way that the sun rises, plenty of light streams in through the windows in the morning."

Rylla turned to face him, her expression filled with wonder. "How? How is this possible? I didn't think these were for sale."

"They are if you know who to talk to. Turns out King Dardon no longer has need for these mills since he has his own on the outskirts of his castle; plus, they've been abandoned for years. By royal decree, he said one could be ours for the right price."

Rylla's eyes widened. "For the right price?"

Caz smiled. "The king offered me a position." He saw Rylla's brows push together and tried not to laugh. She looked adorable when she was confused "He's needed an extra stable hand for some time now. Said I could keep some horses here and turn some of the old mills into stables. Apparently he liked what he saw when I led Rembrandt to his gates. What can I say? The man knows a good horse when he sees one."

"Caz." Rylla placed a hand on his arm. His heart sped. He half feared she hated everything.

"I don't know what to say," she said, sniffling.

Blast. She's crying!

"What's wrong?" Caz asked, cupping her chin. He tried reading her expression, but she looked away. "Are you unhappy?" His heart twisted inside his chest. Anything but that.

"Unhappy?" Her head shot up, tears glistening in her eyes. "How could I possibly be unhappy when you've given me so much? When you've given me the world?"

A wave of relief washed over him, an invisible weight lifting from his shoulders. "So you like it then?"

"I *love* it." She wiped her eyes. "But I love the man who did this for me even more. I don't know how I'll ever thank him." She wrapped her arms around his neck and pecked him on the lips.

"If you keep doing that, I'm sure he'd definitely call it even." Caz winked, scooping her up in his arms.

He spun her around their kitchen, missing the strings from earlier. But with the windows open, the cool night breeze brought with it the sound of windchimes tinkering in the nearby trees. Nature was music in itself. He couldn't keep from humming along.

Rylla laughed and smiled so wide she was the sun itself.

Caz reveled in her happiness. He

leaned in and pressed his forehead against hers. "Welcome home, Mrs. Dumount. Welcome home."

The End.

Author's Note

This story took me by surprise; I had no intentions of writing it any time soon. But one morning, my characters "revisited" me while I was getting ready for the day, and I couldn't keep their voices out of my head.

Not audible voices, mind you (and thank the Lord for that), just dialogue and some scenes.

After writing *The Earth-Treader*, something still felt like it was missing. What happened to Finn after Rylla defeated Lord Brennigan? What about Elowen and Jovin? Uwan? Moo, Fang, and the Great Owl?

Though I was happy Caz asked Rylla to marry him, we never saw what life was like for them thereafter.

So I figured, "Why not now?" After two years of penning my debut, I finally felt like I could do these beloved characters justice once again.

My hope is that this sweet short story gives you some closure, and perhaps, encourages you to revisit the beginning pages of Rylla's quest once more.

Acknowledgements

I want to thank anyone who read *The Earth-Treader*, some of whom inspired me to write an epilogue in the first place.

Thank you, Rachael Crisanti, Tara Koch, Jordan Taylor Nilan, Caitlin Miller, Erin Phillips, Kailey Jessop, Melissa Graham, Anna Deaton, Shanna Crowell, Tiffany Brockmann, Cheyenne van Langevelde, Jane Maree, Amanda Calabro, Frazier Alexander, and my brothers for being early readers and/or huge supporters of my debut. Without your encouragement, I don't know if I would have found the courage to write this story at all.

Thank you, Caitlin Miller, for being

my editor. Your encouragement, kindness, and support mean the world to me, and what a gift to have you as both my dear friend and writing buddy.

Thank you, Erin Phillips and Jordan Taylor Nilan, for being early readers, for giving me encouraging feedback, and for always being the best cheerleaders.

Thank you to my husband for all your support. I love you endlessly. And thank you to our cat, Moo. As always, you're the true star of Rylla's tale.

And lastly, thank you, Jesus. I pray all my words glorify you first and foremost. Without your gift of creativity, this short story wouldn't exist.

Happy reading, everyone!

Alissa J. Zavalianos grew up in New Hampshire and currently lives there with her wonderful husband and their adorable cat Moo. As a child, she always had a love for nature, books, and fairy tales, and as she grew older, that love bloomed all the more. Alissa loves Jesus and is inspired by birds, mountains, castles, Tolkien, Lewis, and the way a cold breath of wind feels on her bare toes.

Feel free to follow Alissa on her website https://alissazav.wixsite.com/website and on Instagram @authoralissajzavalianos.

The Earthen-Crest Kingdoms #1

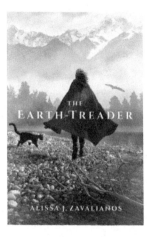

Read where it all began…
Embark with Rylla on her quest to save
her kingdoms, and meet a host of
characters along the way!

GARFIELD
A TAIL OF TWO KITTIES

Novelization by Michael Anthony Steele
Based on the motion picture screenplay
Based on characters created by Jim Davis

SCHOLASTIC INC.

New York   Toronto   London   Auckland   Sydney

Mexico City   New Delhi   Hong Kong   Buenos Aires

TM and © 2006 Twentieth Century Fox Film Corporation. All rights reserved.
"GARFIELD" and GARFIELD Characters: TM & © Paws Incorporated. All rights reserved.
Published by Scholastic Inc. All rights reserved. SCHOLASTIC and associated
logos are trademarks and/or registered trademarks of Scholastic Inc.

ISBN 0-439-87395-9

12 11 10 9 8 7 6 5 4 3 2   6 7 8 9 10/0

Designed by Chris Long & Henry Ng
Printed in the U.S.A.
First printing, June 2006

CHAPTER ONE

Garfield stepped onto an ornate balcony and into the warm sunlight. He raised a front paw and waved to his cheering subjects below. "Thank you," he said. "You're too kind. I love you all."

Servants draped a fur cape over Garfield's shoulders and handed him his sparkling royal scepter. A jewel-encrusted crown was slowly lowered onto his head. The cheering swelled as rose petals floated down from above.

Jon's voice drifted down as well. "I want you to know that you're the most important thing in my life," he said.

Garfield nodded in agreement.

"My life had no meaning before I met you. I was incomplete," Jon continued. "I guess what I'm trying to say is . . . will you marry me?"

Garfield's eyes popped open. He glanced around and saw that he was not on a high balcony addressing his loyal subjects. He was actually lying on his chair. It had all been a dream.

His human, Jon Arbuckle, buzzed around the living room. He was busy lighting candles and sprinkling rose petals over everything. "I want you to be my bride," Jon continued.

Garfield yawned as he slowly rose to his feet. "Marriage?" he asked. "You know, I like you, Jon." He arched his back, stretched his hind legs, and shook his fluffy orange tail. "But not as a spouse. More as a servant, I'd guess you'd say."

Garfield saw his other housemate, Odie, sitting on the ottoman. The small mutt lifted his head, gave his tail a few wags, then put his head back down.

"Odie, could you please excuse us?" Garfield asked. "We're going to need some *alone* time." Odie closed his eyes and went back to sleep.

Jon paused to check himself in the mirror. He wiped a few stray brown hairs from his forehead. "What do you say?" he asked. "You and me. Husband and wife."

Garfield shook his head. "Jon, this is an awfully big step. I could be wrong, but I think there are some legal issues here."

Jon walked past Garfield and knelt in front of a framed photograph on the coffee table. "Liz, just say yes and make me the happiest man in the world."

"Liz?!" yelled Garfield. He marched toward Jon and the picture of his girlfriend. "Liz? She's a girl! Even worse, she's my vet!"

Ding! The oven timer rang in the kitchen. "Hold that thought," Jon said as he got to his feet. He pushed through the kitchen door.

Garfield hopped onto the table and swung his rear toward the picture frame. He knocked it onto the carpet below. "Hold *that* thought."

The cat jumped down and trotted toward the kitchen. He pushed the door open and peeked inside. He watched as Jon pulled a sizzling pan out of the oven. From its wonderful smell, Garfield knew it was Jon's famous braised swordfish. Jon set the pan on the counter to cool, then picked up a bottle of red wine. As he searched for the corkscrew, Garfield smiled.

The cat dashed back into the living room and toward the entertainment center. He reached up and pressed a button on the stereo. The machine clicked and whirred. Garfield spun the volume knob and then spun around himself. A thumping beat rattled the walls, and a blaring electric-guitar riff sliced through the air.

A loud crash erupted from the kitchen, followed by Jon's voice. "GARFIELD!"

Garfield played air guitar as Jon stomped into the living room. Jon's white shirt was covered in red wine. He turned down the volume and switched the music from loud rock to soft classical.

"Man, you've really changed," said Garfield. Jon picked the cat up and carried him toward the kitchen. "Whatever happened to Jon the party monster?" asked Garfield. "Whatever happened to that cool mullet you used to sport?"

Jon pushed Garfield into the kitchen and then closed the door. After Jon was gone, Garfield pulled a small black box from behind his back. He had smoothly slipped it out of Jon's pocket while he was carrying him.

The cat hopped onto the kitchen counter. "That guy doesn't know the meaning of true love." He knelt on one knee and opened the box. A small engagement ring sparkled inside. "You satisfy me like no other," said Garfield. "Will you be mine? I knew you'd say yes! You've made me a very, very happy cat!"

The doorbell rang, and Garfield trotted over to the kitchen pass-through. He peered into the living room in time to see Jon race across it. After pausing to adjust his hair — again — Jon took a deep breath and opened the door.

Standing on the porch was Garfield's veterinarian, Dr. Liz Wilson. Normally, a cat would be shocked to see his veterinarian making a house call. Being poked and prodded in the doctor's office was one thing, but in one's own home, it was downright rude. Luckily, Garfield knew Liz wasn't here to see either him or Odie. Jon and Liz had been dating for quite some time. It was sickening, but it kept Jon happy. And Garfield knew that a happy human is a generous-with-the-food human.

Odie got to his feet and wagged his tail. Garfield sighed and rolled his eyes. "Suck-up."

"Jon, I have incredible news!" said Liz. She began to enter, then stopped. She pointed to his stained shirt. "You've been hurt!"

Jon glanced down. "No, I spilled some wine."

"That's good news." Liz rushed by him. "But this is better. Ready? Guess who's speaking at this year's fund-raiser for the Royal Animal Conservancy?"

"Siegfried and Roy?" Jon joked as he closed the door.

Liz gave him a playful shove. "Come on."

"Just Siegfried?"

Liz grinned and clasped her hands together. "Jane Goodall canceled at the last minute. She's nursing a sick chimp and . . . they asked me!"

"Wow, that's . . . great," said Jon.

"I'm flying to London first thing in the morning," she squealed. "Can you believe it? I still have to pack and . . ." She gazed around the room. "Are those rose petals? And all the candles . . ."

"I guess I have some pretty important news as well," Jon said as he led her toward the chair. Once she sat down, he knelt in front of her. He dug through his pocket. "I . . . uh . . ."

"Yes?" she said. "What's your news?"

"I . . ." Jon stammered as he searched through his other pocket. He finally gave up and sighed. "I've . . . finally house-trained Odie."

"Really?" Liz asked, raising an eyebrow. "I guess that would explain the rose petals." She leaned over and scratched Odie behind the ears. "Who's the smartest dog in all the world?" Odie panted and wagged his tail.

Liz glanced at her watch. "I'd better get going." She stood and walked toward the front door. "I'll give your regards to the Queen. And congratulations on Odie."

Jon followed her. "Thanks," he said. "And congratulations to you, too. They're lucky to have you." Jon kissed her good-bye and watched her leave. "We all are."

Jon sighed and closed the door. "Great," he said. He blew out the candles and shut off the stereo. "She's going to London and I'm stuck with fourteen ounces of swordfish." He pushed through the kitchen door.

Garfield wiped his mouth and glanced down at the mostly eaten fish in the pan. "Uh, make that about three ounces."

Jon's eyes widened. "Garfield?!"

"What?" asked the cat. "I left you the potatoes."

Jon shook his head and plopped down into a chair at the kitchen table. "Oh, never mind. Eat it all. What do I care?" He leaned over and grabbed the ring box from the counter. "It probably wasn't the right moment anyway."

"Exactly," said Garfield as he slurped down the last three ounces of fish. "I thought she'd never leave."

Suddenly, Jon smiled. He sprang to his feet and dashed out of the kitchen. Garfield wiped his mouth and followed him. He watched as Jon dug through the hall closet. He pulled out a large suitcase, unzipped it, and then dove back into the closet.

"That's the ticket," said Garfield. "A nice vacation." He jumped into the suitcase. "Somewhere with big, fluffy beds and twenty-four-hour room service!"

Jon removed an overcoat from the closet and tossed it toward the case. It draped over Garfield. "Can you imagine the look on Liz's face when I just show up in London?"

"London?" asked Garfield. He pulled the coat from his head. "Excuse me? We're surprising the *L-word* in London?" He shook his head. "Oh, you poor sap."

Jon laughed as he picked up Garfield and set him on the sofa. Then he grabbed the suitcase and carried it upstairs.

Garfield hopped off the sofa and trotted upstairs after him. "Well, not to worry, Little Jon. After I save you from this nutty marriage thing, we'll still have time to sample that world-renowned British cuisine." He followed Jon into the bedroom and watched him pack. "You do know the English invented the muffin, right?"

CHAPTER TWO

The next morning, Garfield and Odie sat in the backseat as Jon pulled out of their driveway. They sat on each side of a stack of packed suitcases. The car picked up speed as they pulled out of the cul-de-sac. Then Odie stuck his head out the window. His long tongue flapped in the breeze.

"Road trip!" shouted Garfield as he looked out the opposite window. Then he yawned and slumped down on the seat. "Wake me when we get there."

Garfield closed his eyes and dreamed of England. He imagined he was a king in a grand castle and all he did was lie around all day, eating and sleeping, sleeping and eating. Life was good.

"Come on, guys. We're here," announced Jon.

Garfield stood, arched his back, and yawned. "England already?" He rubbed his eyes and gazed out the window. "That was a short flight."

Garfield was struck with a familiar sight . . . an all-*too*-familiar sight. "Wait a minute," he said. "England looks a lot like . . . the Westmore Veterinary Clinic and Kennel! What are we doing here?"

The next thing Garfield knew, he and Odie were locked in a large cage in a back room of the clinic. They were surrounded by several other cages filled with cats and dogs. Even over the loud barking, Garfield could still hear Jon's voice outside in the waiting room.

"I've never left Garfield in a kennel before," said Jon. "I hope he doesn't get separation anxiety."

"Nah," replied the clerk. "He's probably fast asleep in his cage right now."

"Jon!" yelled Garfield. "There's been a mistake! You can't leave me here! I have abandonment issues!" He picked up an empty food bowl and ran it across the metal bars. "I deserve better than three hots and a cot! They won't feed me right!" He glanced around the room and saw the other dogs and cats staring at him. "I'll have to use the bathroom in front of everybody!" he continued. "I'll get beat down in the exercise yard! Did I mention they won't feed me right? Jon!!!"

Garfield slammed the bowl against the cage and the door gently swung open. "Oh," he said. Odie barked and wagged his tail proudly.

Ignoring his moronic cellmate, Garfield jumped onto the floor and dashed across the room. "Put me in a kennel, will you?" he muttered to himself. He hopped onto a windowsill and pawed at the glass. The window swung out and the pudgy cat squeezed through the small opening.

"This Liz thing is getting out of hand," said Garfield as he ran to Jon's car. "What does he think I am, some kind of *pet*?" Garfield crouched, then leaped toward the open car window. "Where Jon goes, I go!"

He flew through the window and landed on the backseat. Garfield unzipped one of the suitcases and pulled out some clothes. He shoved the clothes under the seat, then crammed himself inside the suitcase. "England, or bust!"

Garfield almost had the zipper shut when he heard whimpering nearby. He climbed out of the bag and poked his head through the window. Odie sat on the ground beside the car. "Beat it, Odie," Garfield ordered. The little dog didn't move. "Go back inside and get a flea dip and a manicure." Still nothing. "I tell you what," said Garfield. "Spare no expense. Get the deluxe package and have a brain installed."

Odie barked, then put his head down. He looked up at Garfield with big sad eyes. Garfield sighed. "Oh, all right. Come on." He moved aside and Odie soared through the window and landed on the seat beside him. "But any more whining and you're on the next plane home." Garfield pulled more clothes from the bag to make room for Odie. "And don't drool on me!"

CHAPTER THREE

Lord Dargis took a deep breath and pushed away from the side of the pool. The cool water enveloped him as he gracefully swam toward the other side. Halfway across, he spun onto his back and gazed at Carlyle Castle. The grand building stretched high toward the sky and sprawled across manicured grounds. Dargis couldn't help but smile. Today was the best day of his life. Today, he would own it all.

The lord took another deep breath and spun once more. He dove toward the bottom of the pool, finishing his lap underwater. There, in complete and utter privacy, he laughed as hard as he could. He didn't want anyone to see him, because he wasn't supposed to be happy. The previous owner of Carlyle Castle had recently passed away. She was Lady Eleanor. She was also Lord Dargis's aunt. No, it wouldn't do for anyone in England to see him so utterly delighted.

Dargis used the last of his air for one more silent belly laugh. As he swam back up to the surface, in his mind he was already swimming through his newfound wealth. *I own it all,* he thought. *The estate! The huge tracts of land!* He was almost at the surface. *The cars, the antique furniture, the jewels!* Dargis's head came out of the water, and he inhaled sharply. *The duck . . .*

With water dripping from his wavy hair, Dargis found himself face-to-face with a wild duck. The beast simply floated there and stared at him with two black eyes. Finally, it let out a loud quack.

"Smitheeeeeee!" screamed Dargis. Frightened, the duck flapped its wings to escape. Before it flew off, however, it repeatedly slapped the lord in the face with its wet feathers.

Lord Dargis heard clicking on concrete. He spun and saw Smithee, the family butler. "There was a duck in the pool, Smithee," he barked. "A *duck!*"

"A duck, sir?" asked Smithee. The older gentleman's expression didn't change. He remained as formal as his dark pressed suit. He held out a lush white robe.

"Yes, a *duck!*" the lord yelled as he stomped out of the water. "A filthy wild animal soaking himself in my pool." He ripped the robe from the butler's hands. "What do you plan on doing about this?"

"I shall . . . speak to the duck, sir?" said Smithee, with raised eyebrows.

"Don't mock me, Smithee," Dargis growled. He pulled on the robe and tied it shut around his midsection. "Have the pool skimmed, drained, and disinfected immediately."

"It will be the centerpiece of my day," Smithee replied, giving a slight bow. "And, oh, yes. The solicitors are here for the reading of Lady Eleanor's will."

That news made Dargis feel a bit better. "Excellent." He traipsed toward the bathhouse. "Moments from now, *I* will be the master of this estate." He paused and looked over the grounds. He saw the duck peering back at him from behind a bush. "And from this day forward," he yelled, "Things will be run my way!"

I Claudius scurried through the grass as fast as his four little paws would carry him. The tiny mouse dashed straight for the group of animals in the middle of the yard.

The Scottish hare waved him over. "Hurry up," said McBunny. "They're read'n the bleed'n will!"

As the mouse approached, one of the two ducks tucked her head under a wing. "I can't watch," said Eenie. "If Lord Dargis gets the estate, all is lost!"

"We must remain calm," said her sister, Meenie. Her feathers were almost dry after her dip in the pool with that dreadful man. "Cleansing breath. In . . . out. In . . . out. In . . ." She flapped her wings wildly. "Oh, rubbish! This is no time for breathing. We're doomed!"

"You cowards disgust me," said Christophe. The goose nudged Meenie with his long bill. "Have you no skeletal structure?"

"Let him try something," Nigel added. The little ferret stood on his hind legs. He boxed at the air with his little paws. "I, for one, will not be intimidated!"

A large Spanish bull lumbered toward the group. "*Sí, que bueno.*" Bolero laughed. "We have Veen Diesel here to protect us." He turned his large black snout to the hare. "Is there any hope, McBunny?"

The hare's ears perked up. "Aye, there's always hope, Bolero." He patted I Claudius on the back. "Don't forget, we field animals will have a man on the inside to tell us what's what."

The little mouse stood proudly and raised a paw above his head. "But soft, I must needs lend an ear!" he said dramatically. "The fate of the estate I'll overhear!" With a flourish of his thin tail, I Claudius spun and dashed for the estate.

"*Mon Dieu!* A big help he's going to be," grumbled Christophe.

The tiny mouse darted toward one of the back windows and slipped into a crack between two large stones. He scurried down a tiny tunnel, climbed up a pipe, and then scampered along a thin support beam. After a few more twists and turns, he ran toward a thin shaft of light. He squirmed through a tiny crack and found himself standing on a bookshelf in the castle's drawing room.

The large room was decorated much like the rest of the castle. Colorful paintings, ancient tapestries, and fierce-looking weapons adorned the walls. Several pieces of ornate antique furniture were scattered throughout the large space.

Today the drawing room was filled with an unusually large number of people. Lady Eleanor's three solicitors sat behind the large oak desk — Mr. Hobbs, Ms. Whitney, and Mr. Greene. They wore serious expressions as Mr. Hobbs read the will. Smithee, the butler, stood nearby. Lord Dargis sat rigid in a chair in the center of the room. His hair was plastered flat against his head, and his mustache neatly trimmed. He wore a dark uniform adorned with gold ropes and a bright red sash. I Claudius thought he looked more pompous than usual.

On the antique settee sat Winston, the English bulldog, and Preston, the macaw, atop his perch. On the red velvet pillow sat a large lump of orange fur.

"'To my devoted Smithee, I make thee caretaker of my estate,'" read Mr. Hobbs. "'Care for my beloved animal friends as you have in the past, and you will always have a home at Carlyle Castle.'"

Smithee gave a slight bow. "Thank you, madam."

"She's dead, Smithee," whispered Dargis. "Stop sucking up."

Hobbs cleared his throat and continued. "'The rest of my worldly possessions, my castle, and the surrounding grounds, I leave to the love of my life. Somebody who was like a son to me . . .'"

Lord Dargis sprang to his feet and performed a grand bow. "Thank you, Aunt Eleanor! Thank you!"

"Let me finish, Master Dargis," interrupted Mr. Hobbs.

Dargis gave a sheepish grin and sat back down. "Sorry. Got a little ahead of myself."

Hobbs returned to the will. "'. . . like a son to me. I leave all my worldly possessions to my beloved kitty, Prince the Twelfth.'"

"Oh, my word!" said Ms. Whitney. Both she and Mr. Greene leaned over and examined the will.

"Good show, Lady Eleanor!" cried a voice from the settee. A large orange cat stood and yawned. He arched his back, stretched his hind legs, and shook his fluffy orange tail. His name was Prince the Twelfth, but he looked exactly like Garfield. "Bless her heart!"

"Can it be?" asked Winston the bulldog. "We are delivered!"

"Thank you, Winston," said Prince with a smile. He stood upright to address the room. "I assure you I take not this mantle lightly. I intend to rule my kingdom with wisdom and valor!"

Both Winston and Preston bowed deeply. "It will be an honor to serve under you, Prince," said Winston.

Dargis leaped to his feet and grabbed the edge of the desk. "But I'm her nephew, her only heir. And she left it all to the *cat*?"

Mr. Hobbs squinted at the will. "Well, she did state that you may stay on at Carlyle Castle and receive your usual fifty pounds a week."

"Fifty pounds?!" exclaimed Dargis.

Mr. Hobbs stuffed the will into his briefcase and got to his feet.

"Upon Prince's passing, after what we assume will be a long and happy life, you will receive the castle, the land, and your title."

Dargis began to object some more, but I Claudius didn't stick around to hear it. He had to tell everyone the glorious news. He slipped back into the hole and darted through the castle walls. When he was outside again, he spotted Nigel the ferret. "The cat has been named the heir!" yelled I Claudius.

Nigel turned and stood on his hind legs. "The cat is shaped like a pear!" he shouted. "Pass it on!"

Swimming in the pool, Eenie turned toward the back of the estate. "The rat has inflamed underwear!" she yelled. "Pass it on!"

Meenie stopped waddling across the lawn and looked toward the lily pond. "Kick the fat off of McBunny's rear!" she shouted. "Pass it on!"

Standing beside the pond, Bolero cocked his head. "*Bueno*," he said, then promptly kicked McBunny into the water.

The little hare coughed and sputtered as he crawled onto the bank. He rubbed his rear with both paws. "Oh, me bloomin' bottom," he whined. "What a bunch of disorganized scalawags!" He turned and saw Christophe swimming up to him. "What do you make of it, goose?"

"I think Prince got the castle," Christophe replied. "And Dargis got the shaft."

CHAPTER FOUR

Bored, thought Garfield. *Bored, bored, bored, bored!*

The suitcase slammed against something for what seemed like the millionth time. Hiding in a cramped space wouldn't have been so bad. After all, he napped for most of the trip, something he was very good at. But hiding in a cramped space next to Odie wasn't such a treat. Garfield didn't know if he'd ever get the smell of dog breath out of his fur.

"Will there be anything else, sir?" asked a man with a British accent.

Garfield peeled back the zipper and peeked outside. The suitcase sat on a bed in a hotel room. The uniformed man with the accent stood next to Jon.

"Yes," Jon replied. He held out a note and a single red rose. "Could you give this to the very pretty lady in room 207?"

The man took the items. "With pleasure, sir."

Jon reached into his pocket and pulled out a coin. "I don't really have the whole British money thing figured out yet," he said. "Is this enough?"

The man took the coin and held it up. "Yes, I'll run straight away and buy a stick of gum." He rolled his eyes and left.

Okay, thought Garfield, *time to get out of this dog breath sauna.* He reached for the zipper, then stopped. Jon would certainly be surprised to see them. After all, he thought he left them at the kennel. *Maybe I should wait for the right moment to spring my surprise.*

"Jon!" Liz shouted as she ran into the hotel room.

"Hello, Liz." Jon leaned against the bureau, trying to act casual. "I had a few hours to kill so I thought I'd pop across the pond."

Liz laughed and hugged him. "I can't believe this!"

Jon squeezed her tightly. "I didn't want you to get too lonely over here. Besides, um . . . you left so suddenly that I never got a chance to talk to you about . . ." He ushered her toward the bed. "Uh . . . why don't you have a seat?"

"Okay," Liz said skeptically. "Is everything all right? You're acting really —"

"I'm fine," Jon interrupted. He sat on the bed next to her and reached into his pocket. "Everything's fine. See, the thing is . . ." Jon struggled to remove something from his pocket. "I have a surprise for you."

This is it! Garfield thought. *This is the perfect time!* He ripped open the zipper and sprang from the suitcase. Odie leaped out and landed on the bed next to him. "Ta-da!" shouted Garfield.

Jon leaped to his feet. "Odie?! Garfield?!"

Liz's eyes widened. "What is this? I can't believe it!" She gave the cat and dog a big hug. "I've got to hand it to you, Jon. This certainly *is* a big surprise."

"No, this wasn't . . ." He looked at the suitcase. "How did you guys get here?"

"It wasn't in first class, that's for sure," Garfield replied. He hopped off the bed. "Now, if you'll excuse me, I'm going to need a litter box and some privacy."

"Garfield, what have you done?" Jon asked. "This isn't a pet-friendly hotel!"

"You know, maybe the hotel is fine and you're just not a pet-friendly owner." Garfield strolled into the bathroom. "Ever think of that?"

Liz got to her feet. "You have to keep them out of sight until you can arrange something with customs," she advised. "They deport foreign dogs in this country!"

Garfield poked his head out of the bathroom. "Deport Odie? I like this country already!"

CHAPTER FIVE

Prince the Twelfth awoke in his royal bedchamber. A beam of morning sunlight washed over his large canopy bed. The pudgy orange cat yawned, rolled over, and tugged a silk cord hanging nearby. Moments later, there was a gentle rapping on his door. Prince let out a sleepy meow, and the door opened. Holding a silver tray, Smithee stepped inside and glided toward the bed.

"Good morning, Prince." The butler removed a silver lid. "Your favorite dish: haggis."

"Ah, lovely," said Prince. He hopped down and sat at a table in front of his large playhouse — an exact miniature replica of Carlyle Castle. As Prince daintily ate breakfast, Smithee poured a few drops of tea into a saucer. Then he added a large helping of milk.

Just like every morning, after Prince finished breakfast, his royal groomers arrived. The large cat sprawled across his massage table as they got to work. They brushed him, massaged him, and gave his coat a slight trim. After that came his royal business. When Prince finished his business, another servant quickly whisked away his ornate silver litter box.

With his morning ritual complete, Prince sauntered down the main staircase. *It's good to be king,* he thought. Normally, this hour was reserved for the royal first nap of the day. But becoming sole ruler of the estate held certain responsibilities. He needed to address his loyal subjects for the first time.

Prince stepped outside to find his royal advisors waiting for him. As Preston flew ahead, Prince and Winston trotted toward the stables. All of his loyal subjects had gathered in the stable yard. Birds, sheep, cows, chickens, ferrets, mice, they all sat waiting patiently for their noble leader.

The large bulldog leaned in as the stable grew closer. "Unfortunately, the animals are divided into separate factions," he whispered. "Beasts of the air quarrel with those on land. Quadrupeds bicker with bipeds. I'm afraid they're in desperate need of your wise counsel. It will take an open heart and a sympathetic ear."

Prince nodded, and Winston loped on ahead. The bulldog hopped onto a wooden platform and held up a paw. The other animals fell silent. Winston cleared his throat, then spoke in a melodic voice. "To all the royal subjects, I give you the new possessor of Carlyle Castle . . . Prince the Twelfth!"

"Hurrah!" cheered the animals. "Hurrah!"

The bulldog stepped aside as Prince stepped up. The animals bowed deeply with respect. The orange cat sat on his haunches and brushed his chest with his paws. He cleared his throat and raised his front paw. "To one and all, I pledge that as long as I reign, you shall continue to have safe haven on the bountiful grounds of Carlyle!"

"Hurrah!" they cheered.

Nigel and Bolero stepped forward. The little ferret bowed again, then pointed at Bolero. "Sire, this crazy bull is forever stepping on the house I built. He put his foot in my living room!" The long rodent balled his tiny paws. "I am not one to take matters into my own fists, but . . ."

"*Mentiras!* Lies!" interrupted Bolero. "He make a booby trap every day. I nearly break my leg, there are so many holes!"

Preston flew onto the stage. The macaw gave a curt bow. "And sire, these commoners congregate entirely too close to the castle. While I draw up plans for a moat, I feel we should institute the one-hundred-yard rule. We house pets need our space!"

"You've got enough space, laddy," shouted McBunny. "Right between your ears!"

All the animals burst into laughter. Prince held up his paw and they silenced themselves once more. "This bickering will not advance your cause," he said. "But . . . your stories move me. Move me to listen with an open heart and a sympathetic ear."

The animals looked at one another with relief. Prince continued, "And so, these helpful words I impart to you: Do unto others as you would have them do unto you. That is all." Prince gave a few more gracious waves as he left the stable yard. All the animals merely stared, their mouths agape.

CHAPTER SIX

Later that morning, Lord Dargis peeked out of the drawing room and glanced down the main corridor. When he was sure no one was around, he slinked out. A large picnic basket in hand, he carefully made his way up the stairs. Once at the top, he peered down the east corridor. There were no signs of Smithee or any of the other servants. *Perfect*, he thought. *No witnesses.*

Dargis bounded down the hallway and burst into Prince's room. He spotted the fat cat lying in bed. The lord grinned and shook the picnic basket. "Hello, my little prince. Beautiful day for a picnic, isn't it?"

Dargis opened the basket and crept toward Prince. "Here, kitty, kitty, kitty." The cat's eyes widened as Dargis shuffled backward. Just before the cat could escape, the lord scooped him up inside the basket. He slammed the lid shut and tucked the basket under his arm.

"What a hoot, eh, Prince?" asked Dargis as he dashed down the stairs. He ran out the back and crossed the estate grounds. As he passed the kennels, Rommel gave a low growl. The large mastiff barked wildly behind chain links. He flung long strands of slobber everywhere.

"Don't worry, old boy," said the lord. "You'll soon be next. Along with the rest of the filthy creatures."

As Dargis hurried to the edge of the estate, his destination came

24

into view — the river Thames. He stepped up to its bank and swung the basket backward. "One, two, three!" He hurled his cargo into the river. *SPLASH!*

The lord chuckled as he watched the basket drift away. The cat was floating off the estate and out of his life forever.

Dargis ran back to the castle and into the study. He picked up the phone and dialed Lady Eleanor's solicitors. While it rang, he closed his eyes. He furrowed his brow and jutted out his lower lip. He had to get into character.

"Hobbs here," said a voice at the other end of the line.

"Hobbs, this is Manfred Dargis," greeted the lord in the most distressed tone he could muster. "Something horrible has happened. It seems that Prince is missing. We've searched everywhere."

"Really?" asked Mr. Hobbs. "This is a rather sudden development, don't you think?"

Dargis paused for a moment, searching for the best answer. Then he smiled. "Actually, it's quite common. The absence or, in this case, the *death* of one's owner can be confusing and disorienting to the feline." He almost laughed. "And why not? Their brains are the size of gumballs. I mean, let's be honest, they might as well be furniture." Dargis grimaced. Perhaps that was too much.

"Still seems fishy to me," said Mr. Hobbs.

"Well, I don't care how it *seems* to you," barked the lord. "Legally, now that he is gone, the title to the Carlyle Estate falls to me. Am I not correct?"

He heard Mr. Hobbs sigh. "I will gather the estate solicitors at the earliest convenience. If Prince does not appear by then, we will do as instructed. Until then, I trust your search will continue?"

Dargis put on his sad face once more. "I'll leave no stone unturned," he assured. "Bye, now." He quickly hung up the phone.

"Prince?" called a voice outside the study. Smithee stepped into the room. He bent down to look under a chair. "Prince? Where could he be?"

Lord Dargis quickly picked up some papers from the desk. He pretended to read them with great interest.

"Sir, have you by any chance seen Prince?" asked the butler. "I can't seem to find him anywhere."

"Oh, dear, has our little orange bundle of joy gone missing?" asked Dargis.

Smithee continued to gaze about the room. "I'm afraid so, sir."

"Well, never mind about that right now." He put down the papers. "I need you to run an errand for me in London. Pick up my new suits at Willoughby's."

"Yes, sir," Smithee replied with a small bow. "Right away."

Dargis could hardly keep from laughing before Smithee left the study. When he was sure the butler was out of earshot, the lord grabbed the stack of papers from the desk. He tossed them high into the air. As they floated down, he roared with laughter.

CHAPTER SEVEN

"Some vacation this turned out to be," said Garfield. He paced across the hotel room. Jon and Liz had gone to see the sights. Meanwhile, he and Odie were stuck in the room to see the same four walls. The dog panted as he watched Garfield pace back and forth.

"He said I caused a whole bunch of trouble," growled Garfield. He hopped onto the bed next to Odie. "Well *I* didn't kick me out of my chair! *I* didn't put myself in a kennel. *I* didn't lock myself in a suitcase for seventeen hours." Odie cocked his head. "Okay, I *did* do that," Garfield admitted. "But it was still very stressful — not to mention the fact that I may have sprained my bladder."

Garfield picked up the remote and flipped through the channels once more. "You know, Odie, ever since we got here, Jon's been acting like there's someone else in his life besides me." He turned to Odie. "This vacation is turning out to be no fun at all."

Odie wagged his tail faster. Garfield frowned and pushed the dumb dog off the bed. "Okay," said Garfield, "it's a *little* fun."

Garfield turned his attention back to the television set. He changed the channel and saw two men playing pool. "With this shot," whispered the announcer, "Mr. Flangely finally regains his snooker title, which he lost to Mr. Wickham Stench last year."

Garfield changed the channel three more times and found he was back on the same channel. He pressed the button three *more* times and he still watched the same boring show about a boring game called snooker. "Three miserable channels?" He tossed down the remote. "I thought this place was civilized."

Then the image changed to show two dogs being carried by men in suits. "In other news today," said the announcer, "The Queen's corgis, Milly and Tillie, returned from their world cruise aboard Her Majesty's yacht." The two men carried the pampered pets into a waiting limousine. "The animals are said to have suffered mild seasickness," the announcer continued. "But now they're back to eating the finest calf's liver in the known universe."

Garfield leaned back. "Man, to be a royal pet. To be catered to like that." He swished his orange tail. "To tell your owner whether or not *he'll* be allowed to tag along with *you!*"

Garfield sat up. "That's it!" He hopped off the bed and ran to the door. "Come on, Odie. Who needs him? Let's go see London without Jon!"

Odie barked and ran up to the hotel room door. Once in position, Garfield hopped onto his back, reached up, and turned the doorknob. Garfield jumped down and poked his head into the hallway. The coast was clear. The cat and dog dashed down the corridor and hopped into the service elevator.

After they snuck out of the hotel, Garfield and Odie saw all the sights in London. They saw the huge clock tower, Big Ben. They rode the giant Ferris wheel, the London Eye, and they even watched a soccer game starring the famous soccer player David Beckham.

Beckham wasn't the only celebrity they saw that day. Garfield and Odie visited Windsor Castle, where the Queen lives. There, they caught a glimpse of the famous pets themselves, the Queen's two dogs.

Garfield poked his head through the legs of the tourist onlookers. "Hey, it's those royal corgis!" He watched as they rode by in an ornate carriage. They sat in an older woman's lap. Garfield guessed she was the Queen or something. "So, this is how they roll in the West End!"

Garfield turned to look for his canine companion. "See, that's how you treat a pet, Odie." The dog was nowhere to be found. "Odie?"

Garfield snaked toward the back of the crowd. Once out in the open, he spotted Odie. "Uh-oh." The dog was sniffing the pant leg of one of the palace guards.

The guards in London were world famous for remaining completely motionless while at their posts. No matter how many faces you made at them, or rude noises you squeaked from your armpit, the guards didn't move. And earlier, Garfield had tried them all. Unfortunately, it seemed as if Odie was really going to put them to the test. "Oh, no," said Garfield as he watched the mutt lift his hind leg over the guard's boots.

A moment later, Garfield and Odie tore out of the palace gates. Several angry guards chased after them. Apparently, they were allowed to move when a dumb dog decided to relieve himself on their boots. "Great," said Garfield. "Here I am in the heart of civilization and I'm stuck with the village idiot."

Garfield and Odie quickly lost the guards in the busy London streets. They zigzagged through pedestrians on the sidewalk, took a couple of side streets, and ducked down some alleys. They were about to emerge from an alley and double back to the hotel when something blocked their path. A shiny black car screeched to a stop in front of them.

"This is it," said Garfield. He practiced his speech. "I'm not with him." He pointed to Odie. "He's not even housebroken!"

The driver's door opened and an older gentleman stepped out. He wore a dark suit and had a regal air about him. "Prince!" cried the man. "I've found you! *Quelle fortune!*"

"Mr. Belvedere?" asked Garfield.

The man scooped up Garfield in his arms. "Oh, man. He thinks he knows me," said Garfield. The man squeezed him tightly. "Even worse — he thinks he loves me!"

Garfield tugged a paw out from the man's grip and reached for Odie. "Odie, help me out here! Do something. Attack! Go for his . . . ankles!" The dog simply wagged his tail and panted happily.

31

"I just picked up your favorite treat," said the man. "Mince pie."

Garfield struggled to get free. "Where is that dog?" The man opened the car's back door. "Let me go, let me . . ." He stopped struggling. "Did someone say *pie?*"

Garfield peered into the car and saw a small pie sitting on the back-seat. "Well, I hate to waste a pie." He leaped from the man's arms and landed next to it. The man closed the door and climbed into the driver's seat. "To the hotel, Jeeves," Garfield ordered. "And no need to hurry."

As the car sped along, Garfield picked up the small pie. He inhaled deeply, taking in its wonderful aroma. "Okay, I've ruled out apple, peach, blueberry, and pizza pies," he said. "I have no idea what a mince pie is. It's not on my pie chart."

"Don't worry, Prince," assured the man. "You'll feel better once we get back to Carlyle. Then I plan to spoil you rotten."

"Really?" Garfield leaned back on the soft leather seat. "Well, my good man, spoil me like week-old milk."

CHAPTER EIGHT

Prince the Twelfth carefully climbed up the slimy ladder. He had been floating in the picnic basket for the better part of the day. Fortunately, the basket eventually came to a stop. Unfortunately, it stopped right in the middle of the London sewers. Trying not to inhale too often, Prince had hopped out of the basket and onto a mound of filth. From there, he traveled down an utterly disgusting tunnel until he found the grimy ladder leading up an even grimier wall.

He reached the top and squeezed through a small storm drain. He found himself standing next to a busy London street. "Dear heavens! That was most horrifying," he said. He hugged his arms around himself. "But I'm alive! I'm alive!" He held out his filthy paws. "And I'm covered in waste." He looked away. "Okay, mustn't think about that. I must return to my throne."

A nearby bark drew his attention. "What ho?" he asked as he saw a strange dog sitting on the sidewalk nearby. The dog wagged his tail and gazed at Prince with a somewhat vacant stare. "Oh, indeed, seeing me in this state must be shocking," he said. He walked over to the dog. "I have lost my bearings and you must lead me with all due haste to the Castle of Carlyle." He held up a paw. "But first I require a bath."

The dog simply stared at him. He made no effort whatsoever to assist Prince. In fact, the canine caught sight of his own wagging tail and began to chase it. The odd dog spun in a circle.

"Here, here! Stop this tomfoolery," Prince ordered. "Focus, man. Do you expect me to lick myself?"

Rapid footsteps drew Prince's attention elsewhere. He turned and saw a young man running up to him.

"Garfield? Odie? How did you . . . ?" the man stammered. "What are you doing out here?"

"Garfield?" inquired Prince. "What the devil is a *Garfield?*"

"What am I going to do with you guys?" the man asked in an American accent. "If I lost you here, I'd never forgive myself." He reached down and picked up the dog as well as Prince himself. "From now on, I'm not letting you out of my sight."

"Oh, dear me," cried Prince. "He thinks he knows me." The cat struggled to get free. "Even worse — he thinks he loves me!" He turned to the simpleton dog. "Dog, help me out here. Attack!"

The dog merely lapped at the man's face as he carried both of them down the sidewalk.

CHAPTER NINE

"To a lasting business relationship," said Abby Westminster as she raised her champagne glass.

Lord Dargis lightly tapped his glass against hers. "To Carlyle Resort and Spa!"

Ms. Westminster represented a group of investors who often turned run-down, useless estates into state-of-the-art recreation facilities. Luckily, she had come calling as soon as Lady Eleanor's passing had been announced.

Lord Dargis immediately began to woo her (and her investors' money) into investing in the new Carlyle Estate. He'd even dug out an old model he had commissioned years ago. Everything had been perfectly duplicated — the castle, the stables, the forest, everything. The lord would often pass the time by rearranging its many structures. He dreamed of the day when he could do it for real.

They both sipped champagne and set their glasses on the billiard table next to the model. Dargis pointed to the east end of the grounds. "Now, here I see a state-of-the-art spa, meditation gardens, integrated business center, and squash courts."

The woman adjusted her glasses and leaned in for a closer look.

"Hmm." She pointed toward the stables. "And what of the forest and the barnyard area?"

Dargis smiled as he picked up the barn and tossed it aside. "No woodlands. No barnyard." With a flick of his wrist, he wiped away the tiny trees.

"But what will we do with all of the animals?" asked Ms. Westminster.

Lord Dargis couldn't help but laugh. "Let's just say, those we don't chase off, we can serve to the guests."

"Egads!" whispered I Claudius. "We are undone! We are vanquished!" The little mouse had hidden inside the model of Carlyle Castle and overheard everything. He had to warn the others.

When Dargis and Westminster turned their attention to the south end of the estate, I Claudius dashed out of the model and headed for the corner pocket of the pool table. He ducked inside, slipped through a hole in the net, and dropped to the floor. He scurried across the room toward a tiny hole in one of the baseboards. "Feet, speed this news onward!"

Once outside the castle, he scampered through the grass toward the garden. There he found a group of the estate animals. They were discussing what to do since Prince had disappeared. "Gentlemen, halt, I pray thee," the mouse commanded in a dramatic voice. "I find myself burdened by intelligence most foul. My countenance lies heavy with —"

"Can the double-talk, mouse," barked McBunny. "Speak plainly, man!"

I Claudius sighed. "Okay, fine! We're all toast!"

"My, that *was* quite clear," said Winston.

The little mouse explained what he had heard in the billiard room. "If Dargis gets control of Carlyle, he's going to bounce us out on our butts!"

"Then whatever the cost, we can't let that happen, can we?" assured Winston.

Eenie flapped her wings. "If he would banish Prince, then none of us is safe!" she cried. "I knew something like this would happen. We must run away!"

Nigel leaned back on his haunches. "No! We will stay and fight!" the little ferret said angrily. "We'll make Dargis pay for what he has done!"

"I agree! *Rapido!*" agreed Bolero. He looked around the group. "Does anyone have rabies? Anybody?"

Winston held up a paw. "No, we're not going to run away, or give anyone rabies."

"Winston's right," agreed McBunny. "It's obvious what we must do — organize! We'll set up a picket line. Who wants to be a strike captain?"

"Calm yourselves!" said Winston. "We'll get nowhere this way! We must have order!" Unfortunately, as hard as the bulldog tried, he couldn't stop the other animals from panicking.

CHAPTER TEN

Garfield finished the pie just as the car turned down a long, thin driveway. The cat grabbed his full belly. "Uh, I think I'm going to . . ." He let out a large belch. "Oof, better now."

As the car slowed, Garfield looked out the window. Instead of pulling in front of Jon's hotel, the car approached a large castle. "Hmm. Jeeves, you must have taken a wrong turn." He reached down and picked up a few pie crumbs with his paw. "I guess he's going to stop in here and ask for directions."

The man stopped the car and shut off the engine. He stepped out, walked around, and opened the back door. Garfield hopped out. "Bathroom break?" asked the cat.

"Come on, Prince," said the man. He grabbed some plastic-covered suits and walked toward the front door.

Garfield gazed at the tall castle. He looked at the sweeping grounds around him. "Okay, where am I? And what's with all the 'Prince' stuff?" The man continued to walk away. Garfield trotted after him. "Hey, uh, dude? Come back here."

The man opened a large wooden door and held it open for Garfield. The cat stepped inside and gazed at the giant foyer. A giant chandelier

39

hung over a room filled with paintings and suits of armor. "Wow. This place is like a castle," said Garfield.

"Lord Dargis will be thrilled," said the man as he walked away. He quickly disappeared down a corridor.

Garfield continued to gaze about the hall. "Okay, I'm impressed, but I should get back. . . ." He looked up to find he was alone. "Hello?" The man was nowhere to be seen. "Hey, come on." He turned back to the closed door. "First one back in the limo gets to stick his head out the window."

"Your Highness, thank heavens!" said a voice behind him.

Garfield spun around to see a large bulldog standing a few feet away. The cat immediately sprang into a karate pose. "Back off, pooch. I got skills!"

"You're back and safe — and just in time!" said the dog. "You'll never believe . . ." He cocked his head. "It's me, your trusty servant, Winston."

"Oh, Winston," said Garfield. He slowly put his paws down. "Of course! And how's your momma?"

The bulldog wagged his stumpy tail. "Fine, thank . . ." He took a few steps closer. "Sire, have you experienced some sort of head injury I should know about?"

"No, but I haven't eaten in about twenty minutes," he replied. "So I'm feeling a little weak."

Winston turned sharply and walked away. "Your every need will be addressed, but first, these are troubled times." Garfield followed him. "The animals of your court need to be reassured," continued the bulldog. "I suggest you address your subjects immediately."

"I have subjects?" asked Garfield. "What? Like math and science? What do you say we skip class and I'll meet you in the cafeteria?" The bulldog didn't even crack a smile. Garfield shrugged and continued to follow him.

They made their way outside to the castle's *backyard* — if you can call grass and trees sprawling as far as the eye can see a *backyard*. The bulldog led him toward a humongous barn. Inside the barnyard were all kinds of animals. Sheep, cows, rabbits, ducks, geese . . . Garfield thought that even Old McDonald didn't have so many animals.

As Garfield approached, the animals stopped their murmuring and went rigid. They all bowed in unison. Garfield looked around, shrugged his shoulders, and returned the bow.

"No, sire," whispered Winston. "They bow to *you.*"

Garfield shot up. "I know that. I was just . . ." He looked at his feet. "I thought somebody dropped a quarter." He leaned toward the bulldog and put a paw to his mouth. "Remind me again why I'm here and not at lunch?" he whispered.

"You're to reassure your subjects," Winston whispered back. "Say something . . . comforting. Then we luncheon."

"Reassure, then chow down. Got it," said Garfield.

Winston hopped onto the wooden platform and raised his paws. "Oyez! Oyez! Prince the Twelfth has returned!" The animals cheered as Winston took a step back and gestured for Garfield to join him.

The cat slowly stepped up. He gazed out over the animals. All eyes were on him, and he felt his throat tightening. He didn't know what to say. His mind went completely blank. "Uh . . . hmm . . . when in the course of human events . . ." he said, trying to sound regal. "That is to say . . ." The only thing he could think of was one of his favorite songs. He began to recite the lyrics, "When you wish upon a star, your dreams can take you very far." He began to feel more comfortable. "And when you wish upon a dream, life ain't always what it seems!"

"Oh, yeah?" asked a tall rabbit.

Garfield had to sell it. "Oh, yeah!" He hopped off the stage and began to sing. "You can be a shining star . . . no matter who you are." He danced through the crowd. "Shining bright to see . . . what you can truly be!"

Garfield hopped back onto the stage. Breathing hard, he spread his arms wide. The animals stared back at him, their mouths agape. Silence. They weren't buying it.

The bulldog quickly stepped forward. "Hurrah for Prince the Twelfth!"

"Hurrah!" cheered the animals. "Hurrah!"

* * *

"What was *that*?" asked I Claudius. He watched as Winston ushered Prince toward the castle. The animals gathered close.

"Holy moley," said Nigel.

"What is wrong with Prince?" asked Bolero the bull.

McBunny twitched his nose. "Well, obviously, that feline is not Prince, you idiots."

Winston trotted up to them. "He's not even the cat formerly known as Prince."

Eenie ruffled her feathers. "I knew it was too good to be true!" she said. "That's it, then, we're finished!"

"I can't die this young," cried Meenie. "I haven't even molted yet."

"No one is going to die," reassured Winston. "Look, whoever this cat is, if he can pass for Prince, he may yet save us all from Dargis."

"Aye, the pooch might have something there," agreed McBunny.

"We must do whatever is necessary to keep him on the grounds until the solicitors arrive with the final paperwork," said Winston.

"But if Dargis did away with the real Prince, he'll surely try again with this impostor," added McBunny.

"McBunny is right," agreed Winston. "We must protect this cat at all costs. Our fate relies on it!"

Nigel spread his tiny ferret claws. "If Dargis wants to touch a hair on him, he'll have to get past these!"

Winston rolled his eyes. "Yes, that's surely a powerful deterrent." He turned back to the others. "Remember, no matter what he says or does, as far as we're concerned, that cat is Prince!"

Everyone nodded in agreement.

CHAPTER ELEVEN

Prince the Twelfth sat on the common bed, in a common hotel room, in a *common* hotel. He couldn't believe it. He should have been lounging in his castle, waiting for his second afternoon snack (just after his first afternoon nap).

The hotel porter set the flowers on the table. Jon dropped three coins into his outstretched hand. "This is better, right?" asked Jon.

"Oh, yes," the porter replied sarcastically. "Now I can finally buy that island I've had my eye on." He shook his head and left the room.

The man named Jon ran about the room like an idiot. He quickly adjusted everything the porter brought. He rearranged the flower arrangement, opened the box of chocolates, and spun the bottle of champagne in its ice bucket. Prince had never seen anyone fall over themselves so — unless they were serving him, of course.

Jon dried his palms on his shirt then went to the nightstand. He picked up the phone and nervously dialed. "Hello?" he asked, and then tried to act casual. "Oh, hey, Liz. What? How many for dinner? Five?" He frowned. "Well I thought maybe just you and I could . . ." He listened, then ran a hand through his hair. "Okay. No, it's fine. I'll meet you there."

Jon said good-bye and hung up the phone. He sighed and plopped onto the bed.

Prince edged over to the one they called Odie. "Now listen, my man. Perhaps I wasn't clear before." He pointed to Jon. "Verily, a grave mistake has occurred. I am Prince the Twelfth of Carlyle, and apparently your master thinks I am his cat, Garfield."

Odie stared at him. Then, just as it seemed the dog would reply, he quickly started scratching himself behind the ear.

"This is serious!" snapped Prince. "I fear my subjects will be in grave jeopardy." He clapped twice. "Off we must go! Bring the royal carriage, my kingdom awaits!"

Odie stopped scratching and stared at him again.

"I'm sorry, am I speaking too fast?" asked Prince.

CHAPTER TWELVE

"Thank you very much for coming today," said Lord Dargis. He escorted Ms. Westminster down the main corridor.

"The pleasure was mine," she said. "I think the investors will approve your plans for the *new* Carlyle Estate."

"New and *improved*," he corrected. The lord raised an eyebrow. "Say, I don't suppose there's room in your future for a wealthy duke, is there?"

"Lord Dargis!" The woman giggled and playfully slapped his chest. "I'm afraid I'm already taken."

He poured on the charm. "As am I . . . with you!" They both laughed as he lightly put an arm around her. "Don't mind me. I'm just an incorrigible old . . ." He saw something as they passed the drawing room. ". . . Cat?"

Ms. Westminster cocked her head. "I'm sorry?"

Dargis stared into the drawing room a bit longer. He turned back to Ms. Westminster. "Nothing," he said. He plastered a smile onto his face and placed his hands on her shoulders. He lightly pushed her along. "Well, all right, then. See you next time." He ushered her through the front door. "Do bring the investors by. We'll have a party. Cheerio!"

Before Ms. Westminster could reply, he slammed the door in her face. He turned on his heels and sprinted toward the drawing room. "Smitheeee!" he yelled.

When he got to the room, the butler was just emerging. Dargis poked his head through the doorway. The drawing room was empty. He didn't see who he thought he saw. He grabbed the butler by the elbow. "Smithee, was that Prince I just saw in there?"

The man's eyes lit up. "Yes, sir. Isn't it remarkable? I found him wandering the streets of London as I left Willoughby's."

"Indeed?" asked Dargis. "How extraordinary." He glanced around the corridor. "And where is the little fiend, er ... fellow, at the moment?"

Smithee glanced into the drawing room. "I'm sure I don't know, sir."

Dargis let go of the man's elbow and clapped his hands together. "I'm just going to have a look, then," he said. "Welcome him back, you know."

"Yes, sir," said Smithee. He gave a slight nod and walked away.

Dargis stormed into the drawing room and threw open a desk drawer. He dug around until his fingers closed on something long and cold. He pulled out a sharp letter opener. Dargis ran a finger over the blade. *I'll welcome him back all right.*

CHAPTER THIRTEEN

Garfield strolled across the driveway. Having tea at some castle was fun and all, sort of, but he felt he should be getting back. After all, he was already late for his after-lunch, presnack nap.

Just then, Winston trotted up to him. "Hey, Winston," said Garfield. "I hate to snack and run, but I should probably bounce."

The bulldog gave him a curious look. "Well, of course," he replied. "Hop, skip, or jump if you like. The kingdom is yours."

Garfield waved him away. "No, I mean . . . never mind. I should be getting back to the hotel. So, if the limo's gassed . . ."

Winston ran in front of him. "Leave? What's your hurry, sire?" He turned Garfield back toward the castle. "I've been trying to tell you: This is your home. This castle, yea, this entire estate belongs to you."

"What? This is all mine?" asked Garfield. "You're not yanking my tail here?"

The bulldog straightened his posture. "I assure you, sire, I am quite incapable of humor."

Garfield smiled and placed a paw on his chin. His mind started racing with possibilities.

A few minutes later, he was running across a grand hall. Suits of armor and sculptures on pedestals encircled the huge room. The cat leaped into the air, performed a triple axel, and then came down upon the slick marble floor. He spun in a graceful circle as he skated through the hall. "Ya-hooo!"

He slalomed around the legs of the long dining table and picked up speed. As he neared the wall, he headed straight for a pedestal holding a large bust. Garfield's feet scrambled but he couldn't stop in time. He slammed into the pedestal, knocking it off balance. The bust fell to the floor and shattered. "Oops," he said. "Sorry about that."

"It's all right, sire," reassured Winston. "Remember, everything here is yours."

"And how does that work again?" asked Garfield. He skated down the hall, bumping into another pedestal. Pieces of a shattered antique vase flew around his feet. He turned to Winston. "Mine?"

Winston nodded.

Garfield leaned against the nearby suit of armor. "Everything?"

"Every stick of furniture. Every suit of armor," replied Winston.

Garfield didn't know how that was true, but he did like the thought of it. He wasn't destructive by nature. Breaking things burned too many calories. But it would be nice not to be yelled at when the occasional accident happened.

Garfield looked up at the suit of armor and noticed it leaning to one side. He looked down at his paw and realized that his weight was pushing it over. He pulled his paw away but it was too late. The shiny suit toppled onto another pedestal and slammed into a suit of armor on the other side. "Oops," said Garfield. Then it got worse. The next suit of armor began to topple over. It struck the next one and so on. Soon, the lifeless knights guarding the room were slamming into each other like dominoes.

As the chain reaction reached the entrance to the hall, a large man entered. Garfield hadn't seen him before. He had wavy gray hair and held something long and sharp. His wild eyes locked on Garfield as he took a step inside. Then *BAM!* A suit of armor fell on top of him, pinning him to the ground.

"Smitheeee!" shouted the man.

"And who is that ten pin I just knocked down?" asked Garfield.

Winston quickly ushered Garfield out of the great hall. "Don't mind him. He's harmless." The two stepped over the struggling man, and into the corridor.

"So, tell me, is the kitchen mine, too, by any chance?" asked Garfield.

Garfield stopped breathing when Winston led him into the castle's kitchen. The room was bigger than three of Jon's kitchens. Pots simmered over a giant wood-burning hearth. Loaves of bread and wheels of cheese were stacked everywhere. Fresh herbs hung in baskets, and the open pantry was filled with canned goods. Not only that, but a dozen cooks buzzed about, preparing all kinds of tasty treats.

"Holy shaman! The mother lode!" Garfield whistled with amazement. Feeling a bit dizzy, he placed a paw on Winston's shoulder. "Are you saying I can come in here and eat anything I want? Whenever I want? And no one will yell at me?"

The dog nodded. "Of course, sire. But why go through all that bother when you can just lie in bed and ring for it?"

"*Ring* for it?" Garfield asked. His lower lip trembled. "Okay, now you're going to make me cry."

Winston led Garfield upstairs and down a hallway. The bulldog nudged open a door and stepped aside. "I give you your bedchamber."

Garfield couldn't believe it. His own bedroom! He ran inside and dove onto the large canopy bed. "The ego has landed!" He bounced up and down on the soft mattress. As he rose higher, he flipped backward. "Backflip and a round-off. Oh, no, he's gone directly into a double-twisting Yurchenko!" Garfield bounced so high that he became tangled in the canopy. "Whoa!" It ripped and the cat belly flopped onto the mattress. The silken cloth floated down on top of him. "The dismounts are always the hardest to stick."

Garfield crawled out from under the cloth and noticed a silk cord hanging nearby. "What's this?" he asked.

"That is how you ring, sire," replied Winston. "You pull it whenever you require something."

Garfield twitched his tail with delight. "I want, I pull? I like!"

He wondered what other treats were in his own private bedroom. He looked down and noticed the miniature version of Carlyle Castle. "And what's that?"

"Your playhouse," Winston replied.

Garfield hopped off the bed and ran to the house. "I have a house *inside* a house? P. Diddy doesn't even have that." He crouched and crawled into the miniature entryway. "I wish Jon were here to take notes. This is how you treat a cat!" Before he was completely inside, he became stuck. He swished his tail. "Uh, does this castle make my butt look big?"

"Shall we continue, sire?" asked Winston.

Garfield dislodged himself and followed the dog downstairs. They continued down the main corridor until they came to another doorway.

"At the risk of curiosity killing the cat, namely me," said Garfield, "I still don't understand how all of this became mine."

Winston ushered him into the room. "A picture is sometimes worth a thousand words, my liege."

They entered a long room empty of furniture and full of paintings of all sizes. Garfield saw images of landscapes, castles, and lots and lots of animals.

Winston directed him to a series of special paintings. "These, my lord, are your ancestors, dating back four hundred years."

Garfield couldn't believe it. On the wall above him was painting after painting of . . . him! Of course, they weren't really images of him; they just looked like him. Each one showed an orange cat sitting on the lap of a noble-looking man or woman. As they progressed through the series, the man or woman's manner of clothing changed with the times. The cats, however, did not.

"Wait a minute. I really *am* royalty?" he asked. "All this time I was stuck in a cul-de-sac when a whole kingdom was waiting for me?"

"Yes, and anything you need is only a flick of your tail away," replied Winston. "At Carlyle, the cat is king and I am his . . . *your* obedient servant."

Garfield gave him a playful shove. "Get out of town."

Winston showed Garfield the rest of the castle. There were tons more rooms for snacking and napping, several terraces for snacking and napping in the sun, and a large pool for special poolside snacking and napping. Garfield couldn't believe that all this was his.

At the end of the tour, he decided to put it to the test. For the rest of the day, he lounged in his bedchamber and pulled the silken cord time after time. He watched as servant after servant entered with every kind of snack imaginable. It *was* good to be king.

CHAPTER FOURTEEN

The next morning, Dargis hurtled a dart at the troublesome cat. It stabbed him right in his orange chest. Unfortunately, it was only a painting of Prince. Dargis picked up another dart with one hand while he held the telephone with the other. He listened as Mr. Hobbs droned on and on.

". . . So to that end, I now have the deed and the paperwork in order," Hobbs told him. "I've contacted the other solicitors, and we'll be out there on Monday."

Dargis halted midthrow. "Monday? But I need more time."

"More time?" asked Hobbs. "More time for what?"

"Ah," the lord stammered. "Eh . . . nothing. It's fine."

"Then we'll be out Monday," said Mr. Hobbs. "Unless, by some miracle, Prince returns."

Dargis snarled but kept his voice cheery. "We can only hope, Mr. Hobbs. We can only hope." He turned off the phone and dropped it onto the desk. Then he threw the dart toward the painting. It struck the image of Prince right between the eyes. Dargis smiled.

I Claudius snuck out from under the desk and scurried toward the wall. He ducked into a hole and traveled through the castle walls. He emerged outside to find a few of the animals gathered under Prince's bedroom terrace. The little mouse ran up to Winston.

"Dargis is sure to make a move against the cat," he informed. "And the solicitors will be here Monday."

"Right, good work," said Winston.

Just then, Eenie and Christophe waddled up to the bulldog. As usual, they were squabbling about the lily pond.

"The ducks have always had use of the lily pond four days a week," said Eenie. "The geese are turning on us. I knew it!"

"Imbecile!" honked Christophe. "Zee geese have had the short end of the stick for far too long. We deserve four days of pond usage! *Vive la goose!*"

Winston shook his head. "I don't see why you can't just share the pond."

Preston fluttered down beside them. "Look," he said, extending a wing toward the terrace. Garfield stepped out and held up his paws. "Here we go," Preston smirked. "This ought to be rich."

"Uh, ladies and gentlemen of the jury, royal subjects," said Garfield. "Don't get up or honk or anything. I'll be brief." The cat paused and tried to look regal. "I hate Mondays. I decree that from this day forward, there will be no more Mondays." He ran a claw across his throat. "Off with Monday's head." He paused, looked around, then waved. "That is all. I'll holla' back." The cat disappeared into his bedchamber.

"What's he talking about?" asked Christophe.

"Wait, that's it!" said Eenie. "With Mondays gone, that leaves only six days."

Christophe honked. "Which means we'll both use the pond three days a week."

"That's ridiculous," squawked Preston. "He can't shorten . . ."

Winston reached up and covered the bird's beak. "Never mind," said the bulldog.

Nigel the ferret scampered up to Winston. He whispered something into his ear. "Right," said Winston. "Come on, then."

I Claudius climbed onto Winston's back. The bulldog followed Nigel toward the kennels. They crept up to some bushes and saw Dargis standing in front of Rommel's pen. The lord held a silk pillow with Prince's picture on it. It seemed as if Dargis was making his move.

The man pushed the pillow against the chain-link fence. "Sniffy, sniffy, Rommel." He shook it a bit. "Track the scent! Bad pillow!"

Dargis slowly opened the kennel gate and shoved the pillow inside. The big dog immediately snatched it with his teeth and began to shake it wildly. He held it down with a giant paw and ripped open the fabric with his sharp teeth. He grabbed the pillow with his massive jaws and shook it harder. Feathers, spit, and bits of fabric filled the air.

Dargis smiled. "Okay, boy. I think you're ready."

I Claudius, Winston, and Nigel watched as Dargis grabbed a nearby leash and snapped it to the huge dog's collar.

"I le lete leese the dege ef werl" whispered I Claudius.

Winston slowly backed away from the bushes. "I have an idea," he whispered back.

Winston explained his plan as they hurried to the castle. After they went inside, Nigel split away from Winston and I Claudius. The mouse held tight as he rode the bulldog up the stairs toward Garfield's bed-chamber. Then he hopped down and hid in the corridor as Winston stepped inside.

The little mouse watched as Dargis and Rommel came up the stairs. The lord could barely keep control as the huge dog pulled at the leash. When they reached Garfield's room, Dargis cracked open the door and glanced around.

"Oops," he said as he *accidentally* dropped the leash. The dog pushed through the door and into the bedchamber. "Bon appétit, Rommel." Dargis quietly shut the door and strolled away.

When Dargis was out of sight, I Claudius scampered across the cor-ridor and slipped under the door. The ferocious dog was sniffing all around the room. Meanwhile, Winston sat perfectly calm in the center of Prince's bed.

"Hello, Rommel," greeted Winston.

"Eat kitty!" Rommel replied in a guttural voice.

Winston glanced around and shrugged his shoulders. "No kitty, Rommel." He hopped down and ambled to the open window. "But we have something better to chew on."

Rommel sat down and looked confused. "Uh . . . no kitty?"

"No kitty," answered Winston. He turned to the window. "Nigel, bring Lord Dargis's new trousers, please."

Nigel scurried in from the outside ledge. He dragged along a large pair of trousers. He gave a final tug, then dropped them in front of Winston.

"Thank you, Nigel." Winston grabbed a pant leg in his mouth. "And now, Rommel, how about a tug-of-war?"

The large dog growled and grabbed the other pant leg. Together, the two dogs slowly turned in a circle as they pulled against each other.

Nigel hopped off the windowsill and slinked over to I Claudius. "I tell you, brother, I'd hate to be wearing a pair of those next time Rommel's on the loose!"

CHAPTER FIFTEEN

Lord Dargis whistled as he practically danced down the stairway. He walked down the hallway, then stopped to check his reflection in a mirror. He couldn't help but hum as he adjusted a few stray hairs.

Smithee exited the study with a duster and a few other cleaning supplies. He stopped beside the lord. "You're in good spirits today, sir."

Dargis smiled. "For some reason I feel as though a great burden has been lifted."

"Burden, sir?" asked Smithee.

Dargis turned to leave, then stopped. "Oh, Smithee. I'm inviting Ms. Westminster for tea. It's extremely important that she feel welcome. Bring up a bottle of our best champagne. And I want you to set out the royal china and our finest silver service."

The butler nodded. "Very good, sir." He headed toward the kitchen.

Dargis whistled some more as he made his way to the drawing room. He gracefully sidestepped the desk and plopped into the swivel chair. It spun once, then the lord spun around again just for fun. He stopped himself, then picked up the phone and dialed. While he waited for an answer, he sprang to his feet and glided to the front of the desk. The receptionist answered the phone.

"Yes, Ms. Westminster, please," he said.

While he waited on the line, Dargis leaned back and gazed at the ceiling. When he leaned forward again, he saw Rommel standing in the doorway. "Ah, Rommel. Did we have a nice snack, boy?"

Ms. Westminster answered the phone. "Hello, Ms. Westminster? Lord Dargis here. How are you on this lovely day?" While she answered, he gazed back at the ceiling. He didn't notice the padded footsteps of Rommel charging into the room. He didn't notice the dog growling as it ran straight for him. "Ms. Westminster, I was wondering if you'd like to pop 'round for some —"

Dargis *did* notice as massive jaws bit into his groin. "— *teeeeeeeee-aaaaoooooouuu!*"

CHAPTER SIXTEEN

Prince the Twelfth shifted his weight. He wasn't used to sitting in such hard chairs. He wondered if all English pubs were like this one. It was noisy, smelly, and so very . . . common. He vowed never to enter one again.

He looked over at Odie. The odd dog didn't seem to mind at all. He panted happily as he sat in his chair across from Jon and his girlfriend, Liz. Prince didn't know how long they were supposed to stay here, but he hoped it wouldn't be much longer.

"Isn't this fantastic, Jon?" Liz shouted over the noise.

"Uh, yeah," Jon tentatively agreed, taking in the surroundings. The pub was full of rugby fans, cheering for their hometown team. Jon leaned over to Prince. "Not as romantic as it could be," he whispered. "But it'll do, huh, Garfield?" He held a small black box under the table. He opened it and showed Prince the ring inside.

The cat merely stared at him. "You *do* realize I'm a cat, don't you, sir?"

Liz looked Garfield up and down. "You know, Jon, Garfield doesn't seem quite himself."

"He's fine. Probably has jet lag," Jon said, before taking another sip from his drink and clearing his throat. "So, anyway, what I wanted to ask you —"

Jon was suddenly drowned out by cheers from the crowd — the game was going well. Liz was caught up in the excitement, staring at the TV and cheering, before getting hold of herself and turning back to Jon. "Why am I clapping? I'm sorry, you were saying."

Jon began, "This isn't easy. . . . I was just wondering —"

The waitress interrupted. "Who ordered the pasta?"

"Oh, that's for the kitty," Liz answered.

The cat looked down and was repulsed by what he saw. "What? No haggis?" His dinner seemed to be a sticky, gooey, layered concoction. There was some sort of meat inside, but it was polluted with grease and cheese. Prince pushed the plate away.

Jon's mouth fell open. "Garfield, when have you ever turned your nose up at lasagna?"

Prince looked around and saw that everyone was staring at him, even Odie. He tentatively reached a paw toward the odd meal. "Oh, very well." He pulled off a small portion. "I'll choke down a few morsels." He placed it in his mouth. "Hmm, it does have a unique texture." Prince swirled the food in his mouth. "And it certainly has a rich flavor," he added.

"So, Liz, as I was saying, I've been kinda anxious to ask you something," said Jon. He swallowed hard.

But before Jon could continue, Prince buried his face in the lasagna, sending food flying everywhere as he devoured it. "Mmm. Yum. Delicious!" he said between bites. "Spot on!"

"Garfield! Gross!" Jon shouted at him, but Prince didn't hear a word. He was too busy eating.

"At least his appetite is back," Liz said, as she tried to shield herself from the lasagna fallout.

Prince lifted his head from the plate. He was wild-eyed and completely smothered in gooey, dripping lasagna. "Must have another portion!"

"I'll get some more napkins," Jon said, and walked toward the bar. Prince followed right behind him, holding up his empty bowl.

"Please, sir, may I have some more?" said the cat.

Jon looked down at Prince, then over at Liz. She had joined the crowd of fans and was watching the rugby game, cheering. "Waitress. Can I get some of that lasagna to go?" he asked with a sigh.

CHAPTER SEVENTEEN

Garfield trotted into the grand hall and hopped up to the table. "Enough room service," he said. "Let's get down to some royal eating." Sparkling silverware and fresh-cut flowers sat on a bright linen tablecloth covering a very long dining table. "Now *this* is how a cat is supposed to eat."

Winston sat on the floor beside Garfield as Smithee hurried in with a large silver tray. Steam escaped from under the sides of the big dome that covered the meal. He sat the tray in front of Garfield and whisked away the cover. As Smithee left the room, Garfield closed his eyes and inhaled deeply. He was immediately assaulted by the most pungent odor he'd ever smelled from food.

He looked down to see what he guessed was meat. Several chunks of the unidentified substance sat in a pool of gravy. "What in the name of Lord Dingleberry is this?" he asked.

"It's your haggis, my lord," Winston replied.

"What is a . . . haggis?" asked Garfield.

"An olio of liver and spleen served in a sleeve of sheep's intestines," said Winston.

"Haggis? Gaggis." Garfield turned his head and pushed the plate away. "What about lasagna? My kingdom for some lasagna!" said Garfield.

65

Winston cocked his head. "I beg your pardon, sire. But what is this *lasagna* you speak of?"

"You've never heard of lasagna?" Garfield hopped off the chair. "Lasagna is God's gift to gastronomy. It's one of the building blocks of life and part of the pasta pyramid! It's the one thing humans got right!"

Winston rolled his eyes. "It sounds wonderful. But I'm afraid we're out of it at the moment."

Garfield put an arm around him. "Sorry, Winston. Not good enough."

The bulldog sighed. "I'll see to it at once, sire." He turned and headed toward the kitchen.

Garfield hopped back into his chair and grabbed a dinner roll. He chewed slowly, waiting patiently while his new servants prepared his dinner. After a few hard rolls, he got up and paced around the table. He looked toward the door, hoping to see someone bring in a hefty plate of lasagna. Nothing. He waited and waited and waited. Still nothing. Finally, he'd had enough. He marched toward the door. What good was it being king if his every whim wasn't attended to? And right now, he *whimmed* for some lasagna!

He made his way to the kitchen, hoping to see someone meeting him with his dinner. The corridors were empty the entire way. When he finally reached his destination, he couldn't believe what he saw.

The large room was packed full of animals running around wildly.

Flour was everywhere, as were milk, cracked eggs, and dumped boxes of pasta. Tomatoes and other vegetables were scattered about as well. Winston sat on a stool and gazed into a sauce-covered cookbook.

"...And now add the ricotta cheese," he instructed. The dog glanced up to see Eenie and Meenie stomping inside a large mixing bowl. "You there, ducks! You're not folding the dough."

"Don't yell at us," quacked Eenie. "We're not the ones who drank all the cooking sherry!"

Garfield saw Nigel stumbling across the counter, singing, "I want to marry a lighthouse keeper who lives by the side of the sea!"

Bolero the bull loped over to where McBunny worked. The gray hare threw several carrots into a saucepot. "What are you doing, McBunny? He no say nothing about carrots."

"Mind your own beeswax, bull!" McBunny barked.

Garfield couldn't stand it any longer. He wasn't about to let this travesty of pasta go on. "Hold it!" Everyone stopped what they were doing and looked up at him. Garfield stepped into the kitchen. "What gives here, Winston?"

The bulldog glanced around nervously. "Er, we're preparing the royal lasagna, sire."

"This isn't lasagna, this is a disaster!" Garfield climbed up a stool and hopped onto the counter. He raised his paws. "All right, all right.

Everybody, take a breath." He paused while everyone took a deep breath. When they exhaled, flour flew everywhere. "Look, you guys have to work together if you're going to reach the great promised land of lasagna." Garfield struck his best regal pose. "We all pitch in, we all pig out. Are you with me?"

Everyone glanced around. "Well, what have we got to lose?" asked Eenie.

"That's the spirit!" Garfield clapped his paws together. "Chickens, bring the eggs! Cows, bring the milk!" He looked around. "Uh . . . Flour bringers, bring the flour, and so on. Let's get this party started!"

Under Garfield's direction, the animals began to work together as a team. He even brought in more field animals to help. The chickens rolled eggs from the refrigerator. McBunny plopped several tomatoes into a giant tub, where the sheep crushed them. And Bolero used his long horns to switch on the oven. Garfield had them working to make the perfect lasagna.

Preston flew into the kitchen and landed on a high shelf. "What is the meaning of this? What are *they* doing in the castle?"

Garfield slid past Preston on a knight's large breastplate. "They're cookin', baby! Yeah!"

Two cows carried in buckets of milk. A pig sat in a pan full of olives to make olive oil, and several ducklings churned butter. When all the

68

ingredients were complete, Garfield showed them how to assemble the perfect lasagna. They arranged the layered masterpiece on the huge breastplate and slid it into the oven.

When the lasagna was finished, everyone gathered in the grand hall for a pasta feast. They each had their own place setting and a slice of lasagna in front of them. However, no one but their generous ruler seemed eager to try it.

Garfield pulled his plate closer. "Ah, come to Papa." He inhaled its rich aroma.

Eenie leaned closer to her plate. "It looks gross. All tomatoey and cheesy . . ."

". . . And runny," added Nigel.

Garfield could see he was losing them. He stood in his chair and cleared his throat. "And now, as your king and official food taster . . ." All eyes were on him. "I command you to eat, drink, and be merry, for tomorrow we may diet!"

The animals grumbled as they took meager bites. "Hmmm. Not as bad as I thought," said Meenie. The duck snapped up another bit. "Wait, this is good!"

Winston chewed his first bite. A long string of cheese dangled from his mouth. "Oh, I say, this *is* rather good!"

"*Delicioso!*" agreed Bolero. He finished off his helping with one more bite. Then the big bull looked at the tray in the center of the table. There was only one slice left. He went for it.

Eenie flapped her wings. "Get your hooves off it, Bolero!" she quacked.

"*Muevese, idiot!*" yelled Bolero.

Nigel hopped onto the table. He guarded the slice with raised paws. "Back off, or you'll feel my wrath!"

Christophe let out a loud honk and jumped onto the table. "Zat's it. The ferret gets it!"

Garfield kept eating as the rest of the animals bickered and fought. It didn't affect his appetite at all. He took another bite and savored all its cheesy goodness. "Well, that lasagna-induced harmony was short lived," he said with a full mouth. "My work here is not yet done."

CHAPTER EIGHTEEN

Odie was having a great vacation! First he enjoyed a fun suitcase ride with Garfield, his best friend in the whole wide world! Then he met a whole *new* best friend who was just like Garfield, except he smelled different and talked funny. And, most important, the hotel bed was at least *twice* as bouncy as the one at home!

After Odie stopped bouncing, he decided to chase his tail a few more times. He finally stopped to catch his breath. That darn tail. He'd catch it someday!

Jon walked in from the bathroom, wearing a shiny black suit and tie. Odie's new friend, Prince, didn't seem to notice. He was lying on his back and holding his tummy. His mouth hung open and a little string of drool hung out.

Jon turned toward Liz and struck a James Bond pose. "Arbuckle. Jon Arbuckle."

"You really like it?" Liz asked him, leaning in to straighten his tie.

"Yeah, it's great. Thanks," he answered with a smile. But as Liz gathered her things to leave, Jon's smile faded a little. "Are you sure I can't go on this castle tour?" he asked. "They won't care if I tag along. Come on, I'm all dressed up."

"It's a conservancy function for speakers only," Liz answered apologetically. "I guess the woman who owned it was a big animal lover. You hang out with the guys. Odie could use a walk. And Garfield could use —" Liz paused as she strained to pull her coat out from under Prince, "some serious ab work. I'll be back soon."

Odie perked up at the word *walk*. He liked walks a lot! He was excited now! He couldn't understand why Jon looked so sad when Liz closed the door behind her. Odie looked over at his new friend, but Prince wasn't showing any signs of energy, either. The cat rolled over and addressed Odie. "Bliss . . . total nirvana," Prince announced. "You have mastered the art of nothingness. Shown me the path to inner peace."

Odie wagged his tail. He was glad Prince was having a good time as well.

Then a smell wafted by Odie's nose. It was a food smell. He had to find out where it was coming from. Odie turned and followed the smell toward Jon's shoulder bag. He shoved his nose into the bag, but he couldn't get to what made the smell. Some folded piece of paper blocked his way.

Prince kept talking. "Odie, my trusted friend, you are my teacher, my master, my guru."

Odie was frustrated. He nuzzled the piece of paper but it wouldn't move. He backed up and barked at it. Maybe *that* would get it to move.

Prince sighed. "After all, what is real? My lands and title — nothing but illusion . . ."

Odie shoved his nose back into the bag and found the bag of treats at the very bottom. He pulled them out and chomped down, catching the paper in his teeth.

"Odie!" Jon shouted, noticing the stolen treats. He chased the dog toward the bed.

Prince was unmoved by the hubbub. He kept speaking, even as Odie jumped over him with the treats. "I know now that true enlightenment comes from television, napping, and lasagna. Plates and plates of —" The cat stopped as his eyes focused on the paper that floated next to him. It had pictures of castles on it. "Castle Tours of England?" he asked. He pointed to one of the pictures. "Good lord! There it is! Carlyle Castle on the upper Thames! Brilliant, Odie!"

Prince leaped from the bed. "Once again you've shown me the light. Now is the time for *action!*"

Jon chased Odie into the bathroom, but it was too late. Odie had already gobbled up most of the treats inside the bag. As he finished chowing down, Odie heard Prince shouting in the other room. "To the battlements!" he cried. "Sound the horns! For king and country!"

Odie ran back just in time to see the cat jump off the hotel room ledge. He sped to the window and saw Prince slide down a drainpipe to the street below.

Jon glanced around the room. "Garfield?" Odie hopped down as Jon raced to the open window. "Garfield!" he yelled.

Odie didn't know why Jon was calling Garfield. He hadn't been around for a while now. Odie was about to bark when he saw movement out of the corner of his eye. It was that shifty tail! Odie growled. Maybe he should try to sneak up on it this time.

"Garfield!" yelled Jon.

CHAPTER NINETEEN

"Well, Ms. Westminster, I've had all of the papers drawn up," Lord Dargis said as he escorted her down the main hallway. He tried his best to hide his small limp. He was still a bit sore where Rommel had bitten him. "We need only to sign them, and then it's on to the ground-breaking!"

"Wonderful," said Ms. Westminster. "I should like to move forward as soon as possible."

Dargis swept his hand in front of them. "Just think — bulldozers and paving machines busily transforming this dump into beautiful luxury condos!" He took her hand. "You and I striding through the centuries of dust like giants, surveying our emerging empire, two proud parents!"

Ms. Westminster jerked her hand out of his. Dargis gave an uncomfortable chuckle. "Er, I'll go check with Smithee to see if tea is ready."

He quickly strode away from her, heading for the back of the estate. As soon as she signed the papers, he would usher her out and continue his hunt for the frustrating feline. That terrible business with Rommel wouldn't deter him. That mangy cat was as good as gone.

Garfield was getting quite good at striking regal poses. He raised one paw and placed the other on his hip, trying his best to look distinguished as he addressed the masses. "Geese brawling with ducks, parrots squawking at rabbits — it's time for drastic measures." He pounded one paw into the other. "I say it's time to whip out the secret weapon of diplomacy and bring unity to the kingdom." He gave a dramatic pause. "It's time for . . . cannonball!"

Garfield ran down the diving board and bounced off the end. He rose high into the air, curled his body into a ball, and then splashed into the pool. He rose to the surface and emerged to roaring cheers.

All the animals were enjoying a first-class, royal pool party. The swimming area was decorated with palm trees, coconuts, and seashells. Ducks and geese splashed about, while cows and chickens lounged by the pool's edge. His loyal subjects were having a wonderful time. More important, they were getting along splendidly.

Nigel climbed onto the diving board. "Stand back!" warned the ferret. "I pack a mad wallop!"

"Do it, *loco*!" yelled Bolero. "You got game, bro!"

Nigel took a running jump and dove off the end of the board. His long body twisted in midair before ending in a tiny splash.

Eenie and Christophe swam by his point of entry. "We rule the pool, goosey!" said Eenie. She held up a wing. "Give me some feathers!"

"Straight up, duck," said Christophe as he slapped her wing with his. "*Formidable!*"

Garfield climbed into his inflatable chair. He threw on his sunglasses and took a sip from his cool drink.

Winston sailed by on his own float. "Brilliant party, sire!"

"Told you I'd make a great king," said Garfield. He pointed to the white gazebo. "Oh, who's idea was the tea and sandwiches? They don't fit the theme, but they were very tasty."

Just then, Dargis exited the back door. Mouth agape, he stared at all the party animals. He crossed to the gazebo and picked up the tray of sandwiches — what was left of the sandwiches. He reached down and grabbed the empty bottle of champagne from the ground. "Filthy monsters!" he shouted.

Bolero lapped up the last few drops of champagne from the concrete. "Bartender, hit me again."

The red-faced man grabbed a nearby rake and leveled it at Bolero. "Get out! Get out of here, you mangy ...." His eyes locked on Garfield. "You!" He ran toward the cat.

"Defense, lad! Defense!" shouted McBunny.

One of the pigs ran in front of Dargis, tripping him. *SLAM!* The man fell right to the ground.

As he got to his feet, Smithee came out of the castle. "Is there a problem, sir?"

"Is there a problem?" echoed Dargis. He gestured behind him. "There's a bull drinking my champagne. Yes, I think that's a 'problem'!"

Winston climbed out of the pool and grabbed the rake handle in his mouth. He quietly spun it around so it lay just behind Dargis's feet.

"I will tend to it, sir," said Smithee.

"Immediately!" Dargis barked. "And we'll have our tea inside!" Smithee nodded and returned to the castle.

Garfield climbed out of the pool and shook the water out of his fur. The man caught sight of him again and his eyes widened. He turned, stepped on the rake, then WHAM! The handle shot up and bashed him in the face. Dargis's eyes crossed just before he fell back to the ground.

Garfield and Winston casually walked away. "Does that guy work for me?" asked Garfield. "If so, he's fired."

"If only it were that simple, sire," said Winston.

As they left, Ms. Westminster exited with Smithee. "Oh, dear, has there been an accident?" she asked.

Smithee gazed down at the unconscious Dargis. "I'm afraid tea will have to be for another day, Ms. Westminster."

CHAPTER TWENTY

Odie thought the vacation was getting better by the minute. Jon took him for another long walk and they went all over the city! They even visited the local police station. The policemen there all wore funny hats. Now they were going on a walk through a great big park. Odie sniffed the base of a tree — he was having a great time!

"Garfield!" Jon yelled again. He had been yelling that for quite a while.

They ambled through the trees a bit longer before coming to a park bench. Jon sat down. "What am I going to do?" He leaned forward and hung his head. "London is so big, Garfield could be anywhere. I just have to find him."

Odie panted and wagged his tail. He was about to lick Jon's hanging hands when he suddenly smelled something. It was coming from a nearby trash can. Odie padded over and put his front paws on the edge. He sniffed again, then barked.

"Get out of there, Odie," Jon scolded.

Odie didn't listen. There was a newspaper resting on top of the trash can. Something about that paper smelled very important. He pawed at the paper, but it wouldn't fall. Suddenly, Odie felt Jon's hands on his side. The man pulled backward.

"Odie, I'm not interested in some old newspaper," he said. "I'm worried about Garfield."

Odie wriggled free from him. He had to get that newspaper. There was something very important about it. He put his paws back on the trash can and barked.

"What is it?" asked Jon. He reached down and unfolded the paper to reveal a large picture of Prince — Garfield's twin — on the front page. His jaw dropped. "You're a genius, Odie!" He began to read. "'Lady Eleanor of Carlyle has left her entire estate to her beloved cat, Prince the Twelfth.' Garfield!"

Odie was still pawing at the trash can. That paper had been hiding a hot dog, and he could almost taste it. He just had to reach a little farther — yes! It fell to the ground and he quickly gobbled it up. This was the best vacation ever!

CHAPTER TWENTY-ONE

"That cat has made a fool of me for the last time," Dargis grumbled as he adjusted the small shield in front of his crotch. When he was certain everything was protected, he turned to face Rommel. The large dog sat at the other end of the great hall. "Now, Rommel, it's quite simple." He pointed to his own chest. "Me ..." Then he pointed to the painting sitting on the floor. It held an image of the cat of Carlyle. "... Prince! You have that, Rommel? Me ... Prince!"

Dargis reached behind him and pulled out a raw steak. "Now, choose wisely, boy." He waved the steak, and the dog barreled across the large room. He snarled and barked as he charged through the painting. "Atta boy, Rommel!" He tossed him the steak. The dog swallowed it in one gulp, then went back to the painting.

Smithee stepped into the room. "Uh ... bad boy, Rommel," Dargis scolded. He grabbed the dog by the collar and ushered him out. "Now run along." Dargis turned back to the butler. "Ah, Smithee, what's on your mind?"

"Mr. Hobbs called," he replied. "Are the solicitors convening again, sir?" The butler glanced down and noticed the small shield.

Dargis quickly turned away and began to untie his special armor. "Oh, it's nothing, just some paperwork." He ripped off the last binding and tossed the shield away. "That reminds me, have you seen our darling Prince today?"

"Yes. He's just having a lie-down," the butler answered.

"Oh, that's nice." Dargis grinned. "Perhaps I'll look in on him." The butler turned to leave but Dargis caught his shoulder. "And, Smithee, when was your last holiday?"

"Holiday?" he asked, then thought for a moment. "Well, I can't remember."

"Seriously, man?" Dargis shook his head. "This is an embarrassing oversight on my part. I insist you take a week off, starting right now."

"But the animals . . ." Smithee began.

"Yes, the animals." Dargis ushered him toward the door. "Don't worry. I shall look after them as I would our dearest little Prince."

Smithee smiled. "Well, then, I'll pack immediately. Thank you, sir." The butler turned and hurried away.

Dargis grinned. "The pleasure is all mine."

Liz's speech was a rousing success. Everyone applauded as she left the auditorium and the conservancy officials surrounded her, shouting compliments. "Bravo!" one of them exclaimed. "Thank you so much!"

"No, thank *you,*" she said, excusing herself.

A hotel clerk stood nearby, waving a letter to catch her attention. "Excuse me, miss, I have a message for you," he explained.

Liz grabbed the note. It was from Jon, and he had written it in a hurry. Garfield was missing again, but this time Jon had a lead. And he needed her help!

CHAPTER TWENTY-TWO

As Garfield walked down the west corridor, he tapped a button on his digital organizer. His daily checklist appeared on the screen. "Let's see ... sleep in until noon? Check. Royal lunch ... royal snack ... royal nap ... I'm right on schedule." He pressed the RECORD button and held the unit near his mouth. "Consult kitchen about upgrading the royal desserts." He thought a moment. "Okay, that's a priority. Let's see ... and sign a decree making Wednesday a day of naps." He switched off the recorder. "Wow, running a monarchy is exhausting."

He slid down the banister and landed in the main hallway. He hummed happily as he made his way to the main hall. However, as he passed the drawing room, he heard voices. He stopped outside the open doorway and listened.

"Preston, calm yourself," said Winston. "We are only doing what is best for all."

"How much longer must we sustain this charade?" asked the macaw. "I can't believe this cat is so stupid as to think he's actually royalty!"

Garfield gasped. He wasn't really royalty?

"Well, he does," replied Winston. "And house cat or not, we need him."

"What?" Garfield whispered. "House cat?"

"Just have a little patience," said Winston.

84

"Patience?!" squawked Preston. "He's an embarrassment to our whole way of life. Admit it, this buffoon couldn't groom the paws of a *real* king!"

Buffoon? Garfield's ears drooped. He'd heard enough. He quietly slinked back down the corridor.

Garfield wandered aimlessly through the castle. He couldn't believe he had fallen for it. The house. The food. The servants. The food. The snacks. The food. He supposed it had all been too good to be true.

He soon found himself in the castle gallery. Portrait after portrait of *real* royal cats stared down at him. Garfield supposed they were right. He wasn't anybody special. He really was just a house cat.

He stopped in front of one painting and noticed something odd. The same orange cat looked down on him. However, the cat in the painting sat in the lap of someone who looked familiar. Then it hit him. The man in the painting looked a little like Jon. Garfield's imagination did the rest. The man's face slowly morphed into Jon's face.

"Jon!" He put his paws on the wall. "Man, I've been such a stupid, selfish cat!" He dashed toward the door. "I've got to find Jon!"

Just as Garfield ran from the room, a gunnysack came down over him. "Gotcha!" said a triumphant voice. Garfield knew that voice. It belonged to that Dargis guy.

Garfield was swooped into the air. "Hey, let me go!"

"Your nine lives are up!" taunted Dargis.

Garfield felt himself being carried somewhere. He extended a claw and tried to cut himself out of the sack. The material was extremely tough. He only managed to make a small hole.

He saw Dargis was carrying him toward the front entryway. The man sprinted through the foyer and flung open the door. Two men and a woman stood outside. They were well dressed and carried briefcases. The man in the middle held his fist in the air as if he was just about to knock.

"Ah, Lord Dargis," said the man.

"Mr. Hobbs!" Dargis yelped. He swung the sack behind his back. "Uh . . . always punctual, eh? I was just putting out the rubbish. Be right back." He slammed the door and ran down the hall.

Garfield struggled to get out, but it was no good. Instead, he peeked through the small hole and saw paintings whiz by. Then they stopped between two of the large paintings. The lord pushed on the wall and part of it swung away from him. Just past the secret door, a stone staircase descended into darkness.

Garfield bounced in his sack as the man carried him down the stairs. When they reached the bottom, he heard metal clanking and then a loud squeak. Garfield felt himself fly through the air, then land on the hard stone floor. When he fought his way out of the sack, he saw Dargis close an iron cell door.

"Perfect, the dungeon!" cried Dargis, his eyes gleaming. "There's more than one way to skin a royal cat!"

Garfield rushed to the iron bars. "Wait! I'm not a royal cat! I'm just a desperate house cat!" The man grinned, then ran back up the stairs. His evil laugh echoed all the way back to Garfield.

Garfield pushed on the iron bars. The door didn't budge. He looked around his tiny cell. There was no way out. It was very dark, damp — everything one would expect of a castle dungeon. Only a thin shaft of sunlight streamed in from a tiny window at the top of the room.

Garfield stared at the ray of light. "I've never been a spiritual cat," he began. "But if I get out of this, I swear I'll change. Cross my heart and hope to shed." He paced back and forth. "I'll stop being selfish. I'll never get mad at Jon. I'll just be happy to see him every day. And I'll never kick Odie again." He thought for a moment. "And I'll . . . I'll never eat lasagna again!" He shook his head. "Okay, maybe that's pushing it."

CHAPTER TWENTY-THREE

Lord Dargis led the three solicitors into the drawing room. "Well! This is indeed a great pleasure." He bowed deeply as they passed. "Mr. Hobbs, Ms. Whitney, Mr. Greene."

"We are so hoping that Prince has returned," said Mr. Hobbs, "and our appearance here today is rendered moot."

Dargis put on his best sad face. "Alas, that is unfortunately not the case." He ushered Mr. Hobbs toward the desk. "I'm afraid there's just no sign of him."

Hobbs shook his head, then opened his briefcase. "Well, then, let's make this official."

Music to my ears, Dargis thought.

Back in the dungeon, Garfield sat against a cold stone wall. He pulled his legs up to his chest and rocked back and forth. "Must ... not ... lose ... focus." He stretched his legs out. "The walls! Closing in! Endless days running into night!" He shivered. "Chilled to the bone. No food. No water." He jerked his head. "Losing ... consciousness ..."

Suddenly, a brick slid out from the wall beside him. It fell to the ground and shattered. "Who dat?" asked Garfield.

I Claudius appeared in the hole. "Winston and I have come to rescue you!"

Garfield smiled as Winston approached the cell. "Oh, thank you!" He flung himself against the bars. "How long have I suffered in this pit of despair?"

"I don't know," replied the mouse. "About fifteen minutes?"

"Oh?" asked Garfield. "Funny, it felt longer."

"Let's get you out of here, Your Royal Highness," said Winston.

Garfield hesitated. "Stuff it, shorty. I know I'm not really a royal cat. I don't know why I believed it in the first place. Maybe I was stupid. Or maybe I just wanted to believe that I was something special."

"But you are," said Winston.

"Oh, please," said Garfield. "You needed someone to fill in for your missing Prince and I fit the fur."

Winston hung his head. "Very well, Garfield. You've seen through our little ruse. But we had to do it." He looked up at the cat. "Lord Dargis disposed of our true Prince so he could inherit Carlyle and destroy our homes! We need your help."

"I can't help you. I'm just a house cat." Garfield's ears drooped. "That's all I am, and it's all I'll ever be. Now, just get me out of here so I can go back to Jon." He sighed. "Even if I have to share him with Liz . . . and give up my chair ... and eat *cat* food." He shuddered. "It's where I belong."

I Claudius ran through the bars and up a broom handle. "But you can't leave us. What about ..."

"Let him go," said Winston.

The little mouse sighed and leaped off the broom. He landed on a rust-encrusted wall sconce. The sconce spun with his weight and made a loud clicking sound. Suddenly, a large stone in Garfield's cell slid to the side. The cat who would be king slinked into the secret escape tunnel.

Garfield traveled through a short passageway and soon found himself outside the castle. He didn't know how, but he had to find his way back to London. He decided to start with the main road leading from the estate. However, not wanting that crazy Dargis to find him, he kept close to the forest tree line.

As Garfield passed a particularly large tree, he caught his reflection. *Funny place to keep a mirror,* he thought. He stepped backward and, sure enough, it looked as if someone had stuck a mirror in the large hollow of a tree. He saw a particularly handsome cat staring back at him.

Garfield raised his right paw. His reflection raised the same paw. He raised his left paw, the reflection did the same. Something seemed fishy, though. Garfield performed a quick dance. His reflection danced as well. The reflection even scratched his head just as Garfield did. Then there came a rumbling from Garfield's stomach. He let out a large belch. His reflection recoiled in disgust.

Garfield pointed to the other cat. "Aha! I knew you weren't me!"

The cat wiped his face. "And you must be Garfield," he said.

"How do you know that?" asked Garfield.

The cat stepped out of the hollow tree. "I've lived your life for the past few days."

Garfield's ears perked up. "You were with Jon?"

The cat nodded. "I was. And when I snuck away, he chased me through the streets for hours, never giving up." He poked Garfield in the chest. "Now, that's loyalty. Yes, if ever a man loved a cat, it's your Jon."

Garfield smiled. "Jon loves me? And I can go back to him and everything will be like it was?"

"Yes. You have a good life with him," the cat replied. "You can't trade that for anything."

"It's Prince!" said a voice behind them.

Garfield turned to see the animals running up to them. Winston stepped up and bowed deeply. "Sire! Thank heavens you've returned!"

Prince motioned for him to rise. "Please, we've no time for formalities." He shook Garfield's paw. "Garfield, we thank you for getting us this far, and we wish you a speedy return to your Jon."

"Well, I do miss him," said Garfield. He laughed nervously. "You know,

I was feeling bad about leaving you guys in a bind, but it seems you've got this covered now."

"Indeed we do," agreed Prince. He turned back to the animals and raised his paws over his head. "Come, my merry men! Take heart! Before the day is done, Dargis will taste my steel! Stand with me, and in future, they will write epic poems of our triumph!"

Garfield heard a few groans in the crowd. The animals didn't cheer like they did for him. Instead, they simply glanced around at one another.

Prince lowered his paws and smiled. "And though my desire is great, my motives pure, no one cat can carry this burden alone." That got their attention. "I need your help, your partnership. If we are to rid ourselves completely of Dargis, we must reveal him as the scoundrel he truly is!"

"Genius!" honked Christophe. "Now, how do we do this thing?"

Prince frowned. "Uh, I don't have the details of the plan formulated yet...."

"Well, your appearance in the castle would put a few dents in *his* plan," suggested Garfield.

Preston ruffled his feathers. "I thought you were leaving," he screeched. "I believe we've had quite enough of your —"

"Quiet, bird!" ordered Prince. "We shall hear no more of your squawking. We shall hear what Garfield has to say."

Winston nodded. "Yes, he is as wise and noble a cat as any we've known."

Garfield's heart swelled. Maybe he wasn't just a normal house cat after all. He stepped forward. "Well, we'd have to get by that psycho dog, Rommel. And in order to do that, everyone has to work together. Remember the lasagna we made?"

"Dees is no time for a heavy Italian meal," said Bolero.

"Yes, but if the portions were small..." added Eenie.

"No, I'm not talking about cooking!" interrupted Garfield.

"Ah, teamwork!" Prince clapped his paws together. "Yes, it is essential to our success!"

Garfield pointed to him. "Exactly." He turned to the others. "Are we ready to do this?"

"Hurrah!" shouted the animals.

CHAPTER TWENTY-FOUR

Garfield peeked around a hedgerow and saw Rommel digging in the garden. The cat swallowed hard, then stepped out into full view. "Oh, Rommel?" he said in a taunting voice. The beast spun his head and bared his fangs. "Who's your daddy?" asked Garfield.

The giant dog loped after Garfield. The pudgy cat dashed back around the hedgerow and tore across the grounds. "Okay, this is where that whole *teamwork* thing is supposed to kick in," he said between breaths.

Rommel's footfalls grew louder behind him. "Eat kitty!" he growled.

Garfield ran a little farther. He could almost smell Rommel's filthy dog breath. The cat cupped his paws around his mouth. "Now!" he shouted.

Eenie, Meenie, and Christophe flew into view. They glided in tight formation just like a fighter squadron. Then, one by one, they broke formation and dive-bombed Rommel, pecking at the beast. The slobbery dog snapped at them but missed every time.

With Rommel distracted, Garfield managed to pull away. But then the birds were gone and the ugly dog poured on the speed. He began to catch up to the orange feline again.

Just as Rommel closed in, Garfield rounded a stone wall. Bolero stood on the other side. The black bull had his head pointed at the ground.

"Okay, this better work!" said Garfield as he ran up Bolero's head. He sprinted up his neck and across his back.

As Rommel rounded the corner, Bolero raised his head and aimed his sharp horns at the dog. The hound skidded to a stop. The black bull snorted once and Rommel took off, out of sight.

"Okay, that was a thing of beauty," said Garfield. He just hoped he bought enough time for Prince to sneak into the castle.

CHAPTER TWENTY-FIVE

Lord Dargis couldn't rush them. He needed the solicitors to sign the estate over to him, but he didn't want to make them suspicious. Therefore, he had offered them something to drink, something to eat, and even a short speech on the late Prince himself. However, Dargis's patience could only take so much. It was time to wrap things up and get down to business. "... And I'd finally like to add that the loss of Prince ... well, I'm not sure any of us will ever get over it. Prince and Carlyle Castle were one." He saw something move just outside the door. "It's almost as if his spirit still ..." Prince casually strolled by. Dargis was speechless.

"His spirit still what, Lord Dargis?" asked Mr. Hobbs.

Lord Dargis moved toward the doorway. "... Uh, roams these grounds." He stopped at the door and spun around. "Would you excuse me for just a ..." He put a hand to his ear. "Do you hear water running? I'll be right back!"

How did he get out? Dargis thought as he closed the door behind him. He ran down the hallway, looking into each room as he passed by. He had to find that cat before anyone spotted it.

To make matters worse, the doorbell rang. The lord ran through the foyer and flung open the door. It was Abby Westminster.

"Lord Dargis. Am I early?" she asked.

"Er, only just, Ms. Westminster, only just," he said as he escorted her in. "Won't you come in? I'm just finishing up something." He steered her away from the drawing room and toward the study. "Won't you wait in the study?"

Dargis opened the study door and saw Prince sitting on the desk. The lord slammed the door. "Oh, no, that won't do." He directed her farther down the hall. "Smithee has been . . . painting in there." He waved a hand in front of his face. "Oh, dear, the fumes!"

"I don't smell anything," said Ms. Westminster.

Dargis laughed nervously. "Oh, you can't smell anything at first. Then, before you know it, you're salsa dancing in your knickers." He lightly shoved her into the billiard room. "Why don't you just wait in here?"

She turned around to say something, but Dargis didn't hear. He slammed the door and ran back to the drawing room. He rounded the corner just in time to see all three solicitors entering the hallway.

"I say, Dargis, are we going to start sometime today?" asked Mr. Hobbs.

Dargis tried to catch his breath. "Absolutely, Mr. Hobbs!" Then he saw Prince again. The fat cat casually strolled behind the solicitors and into the drawing room. "Myaaaa!" yelped Dargis.

"What's the matter?" asked Ms. Whitney.

Dargis shook his head. "The matter with what?"

"You screamed," said Ms. Whitney.

"No, I didn't." He slapped the wall. "Old house, makes noises. Settling, screaming." He pulled on his shirt collar. "Call it what you will. Let's adjourn to the study, shall we?" He guided the group across the hallway and into the next room. "I'll retrieve the paperwork."

Dargis shut the door and sprinted back to the drawing room. He burst in and looked around. "Where are you, you orange devil?" The cat was nowhere to be found.

He ran to the desk to gather the paperwork. To his horror, he saw an ink impression of a cat pawprint. It was stamped right on the dotted line, where *he* was supposed to sign. He glanced up and saw the orange cat sitting in the doorway. Dargis crumpled the piece of paper in a fit of rage.

"That was a waste," said Garfield. "Do you have any idea how much my autograph goes for on eBay?"

Dargis trembled in anger as the cat strolled out of view. He tossed the papers aside and scrambled into the hallway. He glanced around but the cat had disappeared again.

As he strode down the hall, he finally spotted him. The orange cat sat at the top of the main staircase. "Meow," said the cat.

Dargis charged up the stairs. "Here, kitty, kitty . . . come here, you!"

The cat took off down the corridor and ducked into the bedchamber. Dargis tripped on the last step, stumbled to his feet, then followed him in. When he stepped into the room, he saw the fat cat casually lying on the bed.

"We have to stop meeting like this," said Garfield.

"Arrrrrggggh!" yelled Dargis as he dove for him. The cat rolled off the bed at the last second and the canopy dropped onto the angry man. He struggled to free himself but he kept getting more tangled. The orange cat ran out of the room.

Still wrapped in the canopy, Dargis hurried down the stairs. He had to find the wretched creature. As he entered the main corridor, he almost ran into Abby Westminster. "Mr. Dargis, I . . ." She pointed to the cloth wrapped around him. "What is that?"

Dargis pulled at the ripped canopy. "I was chilled . . . and thought a light wrap might do just the trick." He chuckled nervously. Then he saw an orange tail poking out from behind a statue. "There!" he cried.

"'There' what?" asked Ms. Westminster. She turned to look.

Dargis grabbed her by the shoulders and spun her back to face him. "*There* is no reason why you shouldn't have something cold to drink." He shoved her back into the billiard room. "Now back in the room —" He slammed the door.

Dargis looked back at the statue. The tail was still there. He glanced up and saw a mace hanging on the wall. "I'm through playing around, cat!" He grabbed the heavy club and stomped toward the statue. "Nobody makes an idiot out of . . ."

BONG!

As he passed a suit of armor, the shield jutted out and smacked him in the face. Dargis saw double, then crumpled to the floor.

The cat strolled out from behind the statue. "That's going to leave a mark."

As his head cleared, Dargis looked up in time to see the incorrigible cat scramble out a back window. The lord stumbled to his feet and rushed outside. He saw an orange streak as the feline tore across the lawn. With the mace held high, Dargis gave chase. The cat leaped over a small stone wall, disappearing on the other side. The man leaped after him. However, his foot caught on one of the stones. He fell flat on his face.

Lord Dargis looked up and shook his head. He was face-to-face with Rommel. "Oh, this is bad," he said. "This is very, very bad."

CHAPTER TWENTY-SIX

Odie's vacation just got better and better. Jon rented a car and drove them through the countryside. But that wasn't the best part. This was a special car. In this car, Jon sat on the right side as he drove. The car even drove on the right side of the road. Odie got to hang his head out of the left front window. He'd never done that before!

As Jon drove closer to a large building, he slowed the car. He stopped right next to a man waiting at a bus stop. Odie recognized the man. It was the same man who'd picked up Garfield a few days earlier.

"Excuse me?" asked Jon. He pointed to the great big house. "Is that Carlyle Castle?"

"It is," the man replied.

"Well, maybe you can help me," said Jon. He reached into his pocket and pulled out a picture of Garfield. "Do you know a cat who looks like this?"

"Of course," replied the man. "That's Prince. The cat of Carlyle."

"Yeah?" Jon looked at the picture. "Well, it's also Garfield. The cat of the cul-de-sac."

The man looked worried. "I'd better ride up with you. Something seems amiss."

101

Odie hopped into the backseat as the man got in. Odie didn't mind giving up his spot. He was too busy enjoying the view. He hung his head out the window as they drove right up to that great big house. Odie had never been to a house that big. It was as big as a castle. There was no telling how many trees there were in *that* yard.

CHAPTER TWENTY-SEVEN

Garfield hid and watched Lord Dargis run though the back door-way. He slammed the door shut, leaving Rommel snarling outside. The man was out of breath, his clothes were in tatters, and one of his shoes was missing. His sock foot slipped on the marble floor as he walked toward the great hall.

When Dargis was out of sight, Garfield slipped away and ran down the east corridor. He snuck through the back entrance of the grand hall. He was just in time to see Dargis crossing the large room. He headed straight for a wall full of ancient weapons. Prince was there as well. Garfield's twin hid under the long dining table.

Just as the crazed man reached the wall, the solicitors entered. "Ah, there you are . . ." Mr. Hobbs began. His eyes widened. "Good lord, man. Your clothes?"

Dargis didn't even look back. "Indeed, it's been that kind of day," he replied, grabbing a large crossbow from the wall. He made sure the rifle was loaded, then headed back toward the door.

"Master Dargis!" barked Mr. Hobbs. "Explain yourself!"

"I have no choice," he replied with a small chuckle. "That cat just won't die!"

"What did you say?" asked Mr. Greene.

Dargis grabbed the papers from Mr. Hobbs and slammed them onto the dining table. "Therefore, you will sign the deed over to me." He aimed the crossbow at them. "Cat or no cat!"

"Oh, my!" cried Ms. Whitney.

"Sign!" ordered Dargis.

Prince climbed onto a chair and hopped onto the opposite end of the table. "Meow!" said Prince.

Dargis swung the crossbow around. "There you are, you insufferable wretch!" He walked toward the center of the table, aiming at Prince the entire time.

"It's Prince!" yelled Mr. Hobbs. "He's alive!"

"Only for the moment, Mr. Hobbs," said Dargis.

Garfield dashed under the length of the table and hopped onto a chair. Then he casually sat at the opposite end. He tapped a claw on the wooden table. "Excuse me . . ." he said. "Sorry to interrupt your little hostage situation, but all this running around has completely worn me out. I say we break for lunch and pick up where we left off." He raised a paw into the air and looked around. "Who's with me?"

Dargis spun around. "Huh?"

"*Two cats?*" asked Mr. Hobbs.

"That's eighteen lives, for those keeping score," said Garfield.

Dargis shook his head. "But . . . I don't . . ."

"Uh-oh," said Garfield. "He's losing it."

Dargis aimed the weapon at Garfield. "No matter. I've got plenty of ammunition!"

Suddenly, the hall doors burst open. Smithee, Jon, and Odie ran into the room. Odie barked and darted toward Dargis. The little dog jumped up and bit Dargis right on the behind.

"Yiiieeeeeee!" screamed the lord. The crossbow flew from his hands.

Jon ran up and caught the weapon. "I'll take that," he said. He aimed it at Dargis as Odie trotted back to his side.

"It's about time you got here," said Garfield.

"Your lunatic dog bit me on my buttocks!" cried Dargis as he rubbed his backside.

"You threatened my cat," Jon replied.

Dargis put his hands into the air. "All right. Well played." He slowly backed away. "I've most definitely been outmatched." He backed closer to the door. "I'll go quietly, no need to . . ."

Suddenly, Liz rushed into the room. "Jon, I got your message. What . . ."

Dargis grabbed Liz from behind. "Perfect timing," he said, wrapping an arm around her neck.

"Let her go!" Jon ordered.

"Yeah, let me go," Liz added.

The lord grinned. "All in good time." He nodded toward Jon. "Now, if you'll be so kind . . ."

"All right," said Jon. He slowly set the crossbow on the floor. "Don't do anything crazy. Just stay calm."

Dargis turned to the solicitors. "And I'll have those papers now, if you please."

As Mr. Hobbs began to gather the papers, Garfield saw Nigel scurry into the room. The little ferret snuck up behind Dargis and Liz. He looked up at the lord, then back to the cat.

"Go!" ordered Garfield.

Nigel scampered toward Dargis and climbed into his pant leg. "Eyyyaaaaaa!" yelled the lord as Nigel crawled farther up his leg. The man jumped, jerked, and gyrated but he couldn't get the ferret out of his pants.

Liz broke free as Jon charged across the hall. He punched Dargis and the man fell to the floor, unconscious. Nigel quickly slipped out of his pant leg.

Jon shook his hand in pain as Liz ran to him. "That was amazing," she said. She took his bruised fist in her hands. "Are you all right?"

Jon looked at her and smiled. "I've never felt better."

Both Garfield and Prince hopped off the table and jumped onto the antique settee. "That's my boy, Jon," said Garfield.

"Let's not forget my man, Nigel," added Prince.

Preston fluttered down and landed on the settee. "Well done, Garfield! I was rooting for you the whole time, ready to intervene on your behalf at the slightest possible hint of —" Both Garfield and Prince each smacked the bird with a pillow.

Ms. Westminster entered the room, followed by Smithee and two policemen. "You were right, Mr. Hobbs. Lord Dargis was willing to go to any length to get the estate."

"Thank goodness you put him to the test, Ms. Westminster." Mr. Hobbs shook her hand. "It was a pleasure working with you."

Dargis slowly sat up. He looked at her with wide eyes. "You were working for *him* all along?" he asked as he stumbled to his feet. "Traitoress! Jezebel!"

The two officers grabbed Dargis and handcuffed him. "The animals! They're all against me!" he yelled as the officers escorted him out of the room. "You have to believe me!"

"Yeah, what happens at Carlyle Castle stays at Carlyle Castle," said Garfield.

Jon put an arm around Liz. She pointed to the settee. "There are two Garfields?"

"Scary, huh?" asked Jon. "One of them is Prince."

"But which one is Garfield?" asked Liz.

Odie hopped onto the settee with them. He panted and wagged his tail furiously.

"Odie, thank you," Prince said with a slight bow. "You are a hero."

Garfield bowed as well. "Odie . . . you are an imbecile." He promptly shoved Odie off the settee.

Jon and Liz laughed. "Garfield," they said in unison. Liz smiled and put her arms over Jon's shoulders. "You were very brave, you know."

Jon blushed. "Well, the truth is, I've been trying to get up the courage to ask you something all week, but something always stops me." He reached into his right pants pocket. "This time I don't want to let the opportunity slip by." He searched through his left pocket. "Oh, come on . . ."

Garfield hopped off the settee and trotted toward them. He picked up something he saw slip loose during Dargis and Jon's struggle. With the ring box in his mouth, he looked up at Jon. "Looking for something?"

Jon looked down and beamed. He took the box from Garfield's mouth and dropped to one knee. He opened the box and held it up to Liz. "Liz, will you marry me?"

Liz fell to her knees with Jon. "Yes!" She kissed him.

"Don't cry," Garfield told himself. His lower lip trembled. "I promised I wouldn't cry."

The solicitors gathered around Smithee. Mr. Hobbs placed a hand on the butler's shoulder. "In light of Lord Dargis's *exploits*, we've all come to a decision. Smithee, we'd like to make you legal caretaker and proprietor of Carlyle Castle."

"Gentlemen, it would be an honor." The butler bowed very deeply. He rose and then shook Mr. Hobbs's hand. "Thank you very much indeed!"

Winston declared, "Ladies and gentlemen, the castle is ours!"

The rest of the estate animals poured through the entrance. "Hurrah!" they cheered. "Hurrah!"

Garfield slid across the room and landed next to a large boom box. He pressed a button and loud rock music erupted from the speakers. Soon, everyone was dancing. Mr. Hobbs and the solicitors danced. Smithee danced with Prince. All the animals danced. Odie ran to the middle of the floor and danced right along with Garfield.

CHAPTER TWENTY-EIGHT

On the return flight, Garfield and Odie didn't have to ride in a cramped suitcase. They sat in first class right along with Jon and Liz. As the two humans sipped champagne and gazed lovingly into each other's eyes, the two pets did what they did best: Odie took a nap while Garfield finished his second helping of lasagna.

Jon leaned forward and tapped Garfield on the shoulder. "Travel is great, but it sure is nice to be going home, huh, buddy?"

Garfield didn't reply. Instead, he tugged the uniform of a passing flight attendant. When the man stopped in the aisle, the cat held up his empty plate. "Please, sir," he said in a British accent, "I'd like some more."

Jon reached forward and examined the tag around the cat's neck. "Prince?" he asked. "You're Prince?"

"Well then, where's Garfield?" asked Liz.

As the airplane made a giant U-turn in the sky, the real Garfield was back in England. With cape, crown, and scepter, he stepped onto an ornate balcony. He raised a paw and waved to his cheering subjects below. "Thank you," he said. "You're too kind. I love you all!"

The cheering swelled as rose petals drifted down from above. Garfield adjusted his crown and smiled. "Hey, it's good to be the king!"